STARR CREEK

Lazy Fascist Press
PO Box 10065
Portland, OR 97296

www.lazyfascistpress.com

ISBN: 978-1-62105-226-5

STARR CREEK

NATHAN CARSON

Jan 28, 1986 – STS-51-L mission ends 73 seconds after lift-off. Space Shuttle Challenger's lost payload includes the Halley's Comet Experiment Deployable.

Feb 9, 1986 – Halley's comet reaches perihelion during its most recent apparition.

April 26, 1986 – Catastrophic nuclear accident at Chernobyl Nuclear Power Plant.

PROLOGUE

Black blood dripped from the old goat's horns in the campfire light. She could feel eyes upon her. They were not the eyes of the dead man who had lit the fire. He was wrapped in his blanket that smelled of garbage, bleeding freely. She turned her gaze toward what no human eye could see.

"You may drink if you wish," she said. With the care of age, she dropped to front knees and bowed her head. The thing she addressed looked to her like a cluster of mushrooms. But its smell was pure alien meat, unlike anything. Throughout her long life, she'd learned its tastes.

It crept close and cleaned her horns. Its cortina flexed as if with breath. The goat let her hindquarters rest as well. In the flickering warmth, she flared her nostrils and snorted. Her horizontal pupils narrowed as she divined futures from the flames.

"You watched over me when I was just a girl," she said. "How long have you haunted this land?"

It skulked toward the human corpse, the trespasser. "Seventy-six earth years," it said.

The goat's ears perked. She had sensed it when she was young. She could see it now. She had never before heard it speak.

A cold breeze whipped the fire high. A moment later the flames died to glowing embers.

"Something comes for my young," she said. "Unless I breed again, there will be no one left to watch my whelps but you."

The thing flapped its gills when the breeze arose once more. "We may not be here," it said. "Our relief is overdue. When it comes, we will tell it of your kindness. Before the cleansing."

The fire went out completely and both creatures slipped into the night.

1

His mama named him Puppy because she didn't know any better. Puppy liked his name just fine until he was three. That was the first time a stranger laughed. That's when he discovered that Puppy wasn't a proper name, but rather what you call something that you'd *give* a name if you liked it enough to keep it. Mama kept Puppy, but she didn't give him a proper name. By the time she was gone, he'd gotten used to it. Plus it always gave him an excuse to start a fight.

At the rundown Blackberry Tavern, Puppy had a tab. When the bartenders heard his rusted truck rumble up, they'd pour him a pitcher of whatever was going stale and leave him to drink alone. Nobody shot pool with Puppy Tyler. No one asked him to dance. He just drank and grimaced and mumbled to himself. Sometimes he dumped his pockets on the table in a booth, hands scrambling through his belongings but never seeming to find whatever he was looking for.

Under the neon signglow of cheap beer brands, he'd bow forehead to formica and knock the table with gnarled knuckles until he was ready for seconds or seconds again. Eventually he'd fall halfway out of the booth, leave without tipping or saying goodbye. The bartenders kept a red marker tally on a green paper notepad, but the balance was never in the black.

Puppy couldn't sit still unless he was hammered. So he rose early most days, cursing the sun that snuck in through crannies in the old split rafterwood. In the wincing mornings, in that old hand-built house, western sunbeams crawled with tiny golden dustfires. The pinwheel sunlight was only broken momentarily by flickering crickets flitting off to dream til moonlight next. Puppy usually woke in a fit, tense with the acrid taste of morning mouth oozing out. He had a spit spot in a corner of the floor. It was overdue for its annual splash from a bucket of creek water.

Starr Creek ran cold and fast. It slithered down forty miles of wood and field. Snow melted from the coastal mountains that loomed over the grey-green mid-valley. Most days the coast range wore a blanket of clouds. Thunder kept quite more often than not. Chill incessant nightrains gave way to clear days warm enough to thaw more snow and keep the creek clear. Those waters seeped up an oilslick rainbow moonshine of fertilizers and worse before cutting a scar through Puppy's backyard. That creek was his bathtub and playpen six months of the year, when he was a boy. Grown up, Puppy played different.

2

Wednesday, June 18, 1986

Willie's fat fist connected in an uppercut to the gut. A gallon of undigested dry dog food sprayed out of Puppy's mouth on a wave of bile and beer froth. Puppy, hands on knees, hurled a few more times on the scored wood floor. Willie waddled in a circle around him, grinning like a fat cat that forgot its mange long enough to gloat over a wounded baby bird. His greasy black hair shone in the neon light and scintillating fiber optic waterfall wall art. Before Puppy could wipe his lips of dreck a biker boot kicked his ass out the saloon door and into the hungry blue night.

Puppy had driven into the little town of Monroe a few hours prior, truck coasting on fumes, meter on E. He was half-starved, too. He hadn't eaten in two days. It didn't have to be that way, but he couldn't take any chances. He'd lost last time and didn't sit well with humiliation. Those lowlifes had treated him like spoor tweezed out of boot treads with a twig. Puppy eased his liver-spotted pickup into the last parking spot behind the squat, flat-topped cottage. The emergency brake ratcheted up with a dying squeal.

The sign above the wood-bordered tavern door read The Golden Bough. Everyone in town called it The Boog, though, since they found it easier to abbreviate booger than do something abstract like assign a color to a formal gesture. On the flickering, backlit marquee, black letters read:

3RD WED DOG FOOD
EATING CONTEST
9PM WIN $50

The prize was a lot more than what hadn't slipped through the holes in the pockets of Puppy's pants.

The Boog was warm inside, but too crowded. Puppy knew how it felt to sleep all in a pile on a cold winter night, fighting damp drafts with the heat of shivering bodies. But awake on the verge of summer, this was overwhelming. Nowhere to go without brushing some biker's belly, some barmaid's behind, or dropping a drink in a feisty farmer's lap. Puppy wound his way to the sign-up sheet, scratched his name in pencil stub. He poured himself a mug of Oly and settled into a corner to wait his turn.

The jukebox throbbed with a Harryhausen beast battle of charging guitar tussling with writhing saxophone. Both bled each other to death over the march of drums and the crackle and burl of blown speaker blight. Puppy didn't let his beer grow warm, but neither did he fill the gnawing hollow in his belly. A clock on the wall in the shape of Mount St. Helens before it blew read 9:42. The bartender had one long arm and one short one, just like the clock. He used them to upend and pour a bag of Alpo into a police line-up of colored plastic bowls.

One by one, bikers of all sizes, some vested, some bare-chested, took their turn snuffling face first in the dog bowls. They chugged pitchers of beer to choke down the muck. Some dumped the suds in first and ate it like cereal. Others swallowed handfuls like pills. One guy produced a bottle of homemade barbecue sauce from a shoulder holster. When someone called foul and confiscated it, he lurked away, grumbling in surrender. Another guy clamped a clothespin on his bulging, hair-infested nose. Puppy just watched and waited and sipped. He felt his hunger burble and grow.

A vast man named Willie strode up to the bar. Puppy remembered him. Willie was the winner this time last month. The room got quiet. Someone pulled the plug on the jukebox and angled a lampshade like a spotlight. Embroidered on the back of Willie's denim jacket was a harp with angel wings. On the front of his shirt was a black and white cartoon mouse steering an old wooden ship wheel with his squiggly arms. The shirt didn't stretch far enough to cover Willie's navel. His exposed belly hung well past his fly.

The great man picked up a full bowl with both hands. He held it aloft like a crown. After he'd surveyed the crowd, he dipped in a finger, licked it and smiled. Then he slammed the bowl on the bar and took a stool over which his fat ass sagged. He buried his face in one, then a second dog dish until each shone clean. Willie licked his lips when all three

7

bowls clattered empty. Then he reached over the bar and dug into the bag to shove a final fistful into his mouth. When he'd chewed and swallowed, applause erupted around the room. Someone plugged the jukebox back in and blew a quarter on "Eat It," which was still a big hit in Monroe.

The bartender reached into the register and started counting out ten five-dollar bills. Willie reached for them. Just as his pudgy fingers swept them into a stack on the counter, Puppy's hand came down to pin him. Puppy's other hand flagged in the bartender's face, fingers splayed in the universal gesture for "four." The crowed cheered even louder and Puppy lapsed half an inch toward a smile.

The bartender didn't bother to wash or change the bowls. The three that Willie had licked still sat on the counter. A fourth that someone squeamish hadn't been able to finish came back soggy from the sink. The bartender topped them all off with the rest of the bag, then dumped dust crumbles from the bag's bottom over the top. It looked like brown sugar topping but smelled of dirt, hair, and horsemeat. Puppy was too hungry to care and he needed that fifty to make it home.

Halfway through the third bowl, he coughed. The crowd grew silent, then exhaled when he went back to eating. He held his empty mug out and someone overfilled it 'til it spilled. Puppy chugged and chewed. Tears streamed from his eyes. He dug back in, by now doubled down and then some. By the start of the fourth bowl he was full to bursting. His body was in a fit over the cruel trick he'd played on it. And still more pellets scraped down his throat to stack in a pile that reached from intestinal pits to esophageal maw.

Puppy set the fourth bowl upside-down on the bar like

a shot glass. A long, gassy belch erupted from his mouth. He reached for the money and slid it into his rumpled shirt pocket. The room was still dead quiet. He took one step then another toward the front, picking his way around statuesque bikers that flexed in silent judgment. Puppy had just reached the exit when he heard the creak of an old floorboard, saw a shadow engulf his own, and felt Willie's weight behind him.

3

"After carousing in the tavern the whole night through, you exit the Bronze Basilisk and set mailed boot to the crooked, cobbled street. Your horse grazes contentedly in the stable where you left it. In the adjacent stall is a well-groomed Pegasus. What do you do?" asked Allen.

"I piss on the Pegasus," said Bron.

"You what?"

"I piss on it. You said I've been drinking and carousing all night. Obviously I've got to take a leak by now. Whoever parked their Pegasus next to my horse is just showing off anyway. Serves her right."

Kira had been staring out the farmhouse window. The old pane was thicker at the bottom than the top. It blurred the wooded landscape in a way that she liked to smear down with her psyche. She let her mind's eye hang on one silhouette branch before dropping to the next.

"How do you know it belongs to a her?" she asked.

Bron looked over the card table at Kira. He absently stroked a tiny silver pentagram necklace that hung around his neck on a thin leather cord.

"Dudes don't ride Pegasus," he said. "Pegasi?" Allen chuckled to himself. "Ever heard of Perseus?" Bron fired back. "That's only in *Clash of the Titans*. He didn't ride one in the original myths. You're the D.M. Get your facts straight, Alien."

Allen winced. That was his least favorite nickname. It reminded him of his four eyes and crooked teeth. Allen held court at the head of the card table, surrounded by polyhedral dice. He was walled in by folded cardboard screens crisscrossed with battle stats that looked like multiplication tables clumsily mating with astrological star charts. His bony legs were wrapped in ripped jeans. He wore an oversized Dokken shirt that he'd purchased for a quarter at a thrift store, mostly for the sake of irony.

Allen absently rolled dice, checked the results then looked at Bron with an evil glint.

"What's that for?" Bron asked.

"It's your saving throw against magic. Roll 1D6 to see how much damage your wang takes from urinating on a magical beast."

Bron stood up, knocking over his folding chair.

"That's not in the fucking rules!"

Kira was still gazing out the window, watching a distant pickup kick up a dust trail as it raced along Starr Creek Road toward the T at Bellfountain. The truck was moving so fast that it barely braked, fishtailing onto the main road before blazing southward into the forested hills.

When the truck was gone from sight, Kira took a swig of unfiltered apple cider from her local co-op thermos then resumed her absent gnawing on a carob nut cluster. She'd offered to share these snacks at the beginning of the game, but Allen and Bron were teenage boys obsessed with stolen beer, Pop Tarts, and Steakumm. They were however quite gung ho when it came to sharing her psychedelics. Also, both were old enough to drive. She was a year younger than them and required the rides and craved their company.

Every inch of Allen's parents' ranch-style farmhouse was covered in framed watercolor prints, driftwood and dreamcatchers. The television was the centerpiece of the shrine though it only received broadcast signal for three-and-a-half channels. A mess of cables attached the aging set to a well-worn Atari and an enormous top-loading VCR.

But today was one of the longest days of the year. There would be sun glare on the dusty screen for several hours yet. So the trio continued its long-running adventure of the mind.

Occasionally they stepped outside to scrape old roach remnants, rolling the blackened body into the bowl. Discarded brown papers fluttered in the wind like wings plucked from a mortally wounded moth. Pursed lips sucked combustible burnout through a brass pipe. The pipe was screwed together from resin-coated plumbing parts. When the metal got too hot to touch, the three would return inside to continue their quest for a world less mundane.

Kira had designs and lysergic inventory that would make tomorrow a day to remember. But her stock was well hidden in her bedroom in Corvallis. A trip back to town meant begging Bron to drive her there and back again. She picked up a rattling handful of dice and keenly eyed both boys.

"I'm stealing that fucking Pegasus," she said. "Let's ride."

4

Hours later, Bron slammed his floor shifter into third gear and mashed the accelerator to the rain mat. He had spent the better part of a year restoring the '71 Dodge Dart Demon from a rusting hulk to a primer-grey speed machine. The 340 may have been a small block, but outside of cops or nitro-boosted funny cars, he wasn't sweating any local competition.

The straightaway on Bellfountain road was his favorite spot to really open it up. On his right was the silhouette of Mary's Peak, its outline glowing blood red at summer sunset. His right hand blocked the glare since the passenger sun visor didn't reach quite so low. He squinted, locked his left hand on the steering wheel, pushed a black tape with an eggshell label into the cassette deck.

James Hetfield's voice intoned Lovecraft's famous couplet. An immense guitar riff crashed out of the speakers, like ocean waves flooding an ancient city.

The Dart blew past a farmhouse with an orphaned crumbling tower. Soon the open fields were left behind. Bron raced uphill toward the old Airport Road junction, entering the tunnel enclosure of nature's canopy. A great gust from the Demon's passage tore healthy leaves from twisted tree limbs. The leaves swirled like a swarm of bats, careening in all directions and smacking onto the cracked windshield. Bron hit the wipers. They screeched on the dry glass, so he turned up the volume on the stereo. The unpleasant sound drowned beneath the aural grout of chugging metal music.

The brakes were still part of the restoration in progress. Bron jammed down to second gear halfway through the first S-curve that separated dairy farmland from the doctor's property around the bend. The Demon's wheels skidded nimbly around the corner. Bron gave the beast just enough gas to accelerate out of the turn.

Day was turning in. Bron switched on the headlights and caught a gleam in the roadside gravel. He saw Allen's bike ditched outside the pioneer cemetery, so he gave the brakes a test after all.

*

Allen lay flat on the cooling earth, covered in ivy and grave moss. He was muttering to himself, cursing Marnie's name and trying to scrub his mind of painful daydreams. The evening was growing dark and she hadn't shown up yet. This was beyond embarrassing. Just two weeks earlier, on the last day of school, he'd almost worked up the courage to ask her to "go with him." Instead, he'd managed to squeak and blush for her number. Receiving her family's private line in purple marker on the inside dust jacket of his yearbook seemed like victory. From the rotary wall phone in his parents' kitchen, he'd finally mustered the nerve to call her. Her merciless older sister grilled him for what seemed like forever. When Marnie took the phone, she agreed to meet him at the cemetery at sunset. Or at least, it seemed like she had. Maybe he'd heard her wrong.

His plan was to hide and scare her. Allen loved to watch horror movies and stay up late reading Dean Koontz novels. So he figured the best way to impress Marnie would be to shimmy under the ivy that covered the graveyard like a cobweb of green-grey frondescence and try to scare the living shit out of her. The longer he lay there, the more he felt stupid for asking out a freshman, especially one who listened to terrible music and wore a cowboy hat. She really had nothing to offer beyond living nearby and having rich parents and being painfully cute.

Allen was a Dungeon Master and took all the hard classes and had turned down a girl who liked him back in fifth grade because she had B.O. Waiting around for Marnie was clearly beneath him. And night was falling and his foot was asleep from lying on the ground for so long. Just as he rose to stumble out of the graveyard like a zombie, he heard the metal on metal of Bron's bleeding brakes.

*

The gate to the cemetery was barred by a padlock hanging from a rusted chain. But Bron hopped higher fences than this all the time. He looked both ways to make sure no one was watching. He leaned the machete that he kept in his car on the other side of the gate and clambered over. The darkness inside felt ten degrees cooler than the road. Dense trees arched overhead and wept that contagious grey-green moss. Mist curled around obelisks and headstones. Most of those veered at odd angles from a century of shifting earth. The rest of the cold and dark was simply unexplainable. Bron felt a shiver go down his back. He drew the machete out of its sheath and pressed onward.

Allen was crouched behind a teetering marble column. He snickered to himself as Bron's cautious footfalls reached ever closer. At the last possible second, Allen sprang forth. He clutched at Bron's shin with a grasp intended to be both paralyzing and horrifying.

Bron swung the machete. It grazed the finest loose hairs on the top of Allen's head then sank with a dead stop into a crack in the marble column. For a few seconds the two friends trembled in silence, searching for words.

Finally, Allen's aching, shaking knees seemed ready to work again. He rose to his full standing height of 5'4" and peered at the machete, which rested at the same level as his four eyes.

Bron took a deep breath and looked down. Though he stood head and shoulders above, he was only Allen's elder by about six months. Bron shook his head, trying not to think about whether he'd have been tried as an adult for decapitating his best friend.

"Stupid fucker," he said. Then he smiled, baring perfect white teeth with canines that seemed ever so slightly long.

"Sorry man," Allen said. "I thought it would be funny.

I didn't know you were armed. I guess I won my initiative roll this time." Both smirked.

"I never realized how freaky this place is at night," Bron said.

"Yeah. I didn't intend to be here this late. At least...not with you. Hope your machete isn't fucked."

Bron took hold of the handle with both hands and wrested it free of the stone. There was a sizable chip in the blade. He drew his thumb along the jagged steel.

"Battle damage," he said.

Satisfied, he sheathed it and turned to the cracked grave marker. He traced his hand over the words chiseled in the façade.

Pieter Coolen
Nov 9, 1887-Apr 20, 1910

Adelaide Coolen
Mar 27, 1889-Apr 20, 1910

"Wow," Bron said. "They both died on the same day."

"Mhm," Allen said. "All these people died on the same day. It's fucking weird."

They walked a rough figure eight through the ivy, stepping over sunken plots and circuiting graves marked only by wooden crosses or nothing at all. All Dutch settlers. All deceased on April 20, 1910.

"You know what this means, right Allen?"

"Yeah."

They both looked into each other's eyes and exclaimed, "Four-twenty, dude!"

Then Bron put his arm around the shoulders of his diminutive friend and said, "I've got a pipe in the glove box. Let's get out of here."

5

Willie whistled "Turkey in the Straw" as he sauntered around the back of The Boog. Someone with huge balls had parked a rice burner by his hog. He looked left, then right. No one was watching that he could see. Then he bent his knees a bit, fumbled for his fly, and let loose a hot stream on the aerodynamic Hondasaki or whatever.

Across the dark lot, Puppy clenched the wheel of his pickup and gritted his teeth. His mouth still burned with the taste of the gasoline he'd siphoned out of Willie's tank.

Willie shook, then zipped. He mounted his own steed and gave it a few kicks before it finally leapt to life. Still soused from the night's escapades, he struggled a bit to strap on his brain bucket. None of the gang had been happy about losing their God-given freedom, but the helmet law had come nearly ten years back—the same year as *Star Wars*. At this point, there was no sense in risking a ticket.

He pulled the vented gloves over his bulging pig knuckles, revved the engine, and pealed into the night.

Puppy counted to six then started his truck.

Willie rode north on Highway 99. He knew every curve of that road. He wove between the white and yellow lines just to entertain his big bad self. In his side mirror, he glimpsed a single headlamp about a quarter mile behind. Must be one of the boys, he thought; Monroe didn't have motorcycle cops. He gave the throttle a touch more wrist.

The round yellow light behind kept getting closer, though. Someone's in a hurry to get home, thought Willie. Wonder who it is? He revved his engine to give a bit of race and felt the compression sag.

Pretty soon the other bike was right on his ass. Willie crossed into the oncoming lane to let it pass. That's when he realized that he wasn't seeing a bike at all, but rather a truck with one headlight out and one vengeful hillbilly leaning halfway out the driver-side window clutching a crowbar.

Willie knew he could outrun Puppy's tired old rig. He tried to gun his Harley—except the needle on his gas gauge was now deep in the red. At full throttle he was losing speed.

Puppy's forearm flexed as he swung the crowbar wide. It caught the brim of Willie's helmet. Then Puppy locked up the brakes. Willie's weight would easily have broken his arm if he'd held on. Puppy let go the moment he felt Willie disconnect from his bike. The Harley carried on like a ghost had climbed aboard for a wild midnight run. It was a short ride. The bike ran out of road and bounced end over end into a wooded ravine.

Willie was lying on the centerline still trying to unhook

the crowbar from his face. Puppy stomped back around and kicked Willie in the stomach. Then the little man dragged the big man by the crowbar toward the back of his truck.

Each time Willie struggled he got another kick. With all the beer, the hard fall, and the blood in his eye, there wasn't much he could do. Puppy fumbled him up into the bed of the pickup, tied him down with an assortment of rotting bungee cords, and then covered him with a weathered tarp.

As the truck lumbered back into motion, Willie bumped and bled and cursed for a full fifteen minutes. After that he started to pray.

When the truck finally lurched to a stop, Willie tried to recall all the country roads he knew in the mid-valley. Just where might he be after twenty minutes of pavement and another twelve-to-fifteen on gravel? Too many possibilities.

Puppy seemed in no hurry to fetch him once they'd stopped. Time went by and Willie eventually passed out into a painful, dream-haunted sleep.

*

The sky was still dark when Puppy came for him at last. He yanked the tarp off and put a boot on Willie's blubbery chest. He wrapped both hands around the crowbar that was still embedded in Willie's *Stahlhelm*. As Puppy pulled, Willie screamed. The claw end of the crowbar was hooked in the corner of Willie's eye socket, which broke at the same instant as the helmet. Puppy dislodged the bungees from the sides of the truck. With great effort, he drug Willie feet first out of the bed and head first onto the ground.

"You let me go, Puppy dog," Willie said between sobs.

"You know Angel's Harp will come for ya'. Ain't gonna do you no good messing with me."

A kick in the mouth shut him up again. Willie spat out a front tooth. He stuck his tongue in the socket to staunch the blood and said no more.

Puppy propped Willie up against the trunk of a tree and fixed the bungees around it. Again he picked up the crowbar, glowering down at the bleeding bulk who had publicly shamed him two months running. The taste of dog food and gasoline churned his stomach over and he vomited naught but stomach acid bile right onto Willie's wincing, bleeding socket. The eye rolled up at Puppy and burned in the first ray of dawn light. It saw no mercy.

"Now I want you," Puppy said, "to bark like a dog."

6

Bron's Dodge crunched into the long gravel driveway of Allen's parents' place. The muffled sounds of Metallica emanated from within. Thick weed smoke leaked from the cracked rubber window seals. They parked in front of the barn, headlights dying with the engine. Heavy metal doors swung open releasing peals of laughter as Bron and Allen stumbled out.

"So," Allen said with a shit-eating grin and red, puffy eyes. "How is Kira getting out here?"

"Oh fuck," Bron said back. "I think I was supposed to pick her up."

Their minds both reeled in confusion at what to do. That certain flavor of paranoia that only the young or inexperienced Cannabis-smoker tastes sunk into their hearts.

Before they could formulate a plan they heard the distinct lawnmower purr of a Volkswagen bus settle to a stop at the foot of the drive. A door opened and shut then the bus sped on. With her green army surplus jacket, a gallon jug of water, and a backpack slung over one shoulder, came Kira.

She said, "What happened to you, jerk?"

Bron said, "I'm really sorry. I was getting ready to go and I decided to scrape my pipe. You know, so it would be really clean for you guys. And I guess, well, I smoked the resin and…then I just drove straight out here. Oops."

"It's cool," she said. "I hitch all the time. That guy was really nice." Kira shrugged. "I think he lives on a commune out on Starr Creek. That's where I think we should go tomorrow."

"That road is totally haunted," Allen said. "Count me in."

"Cool," they all said together. Then they headed inside to settle down and make a plan. They had found that the best acid trips were strategically mapped out in advance. A bit of structure was a good safety net for all the curveballs reality threw when you chomped down four hits of Gooney Bird or a couple of microdots.

Bron was the oldest and Allen was the Dungeon Master. But Kira was always their trip director. The Acid Queen. No matter how far out they got, she was able to follow a silver cord out of the astral plane and back down to Earth. Thanks to her, none of them had lost a finger or gone to jail. She also took pride in ensuring a constant supply of clean, high quality, strychnine-free blotter, liquid, or caps.

Bron's Demon helped them get around. 'Nuff said.

Allen's access to the wild was a godsend to the two who lived in town. He daydreamed about living in the suburbs and sneaking out the window to meet up with friends on lamplit summer nights. Kira and Bron shook their heads.

They marveled at the starry sky visible from his remote property. The farm was ten miles from any urban place. With no moon they could see the cold x-ray smear of the Milky Way behind even the brightest stars. And young minds on acid just loved to do rail slides down that vast spiral arm.

The walls of Allen's bedroom were covered in posters. H.R. Giger biomechanoids hung by a poolside comic frame full of female Teen Titans in skimpy bikinis. The only wall spared had been hand-painted with dungeon cobble brickwork. A black portal was in the center, unbroken save for a triumvirate of glowing eyes. Yes, this was the bedroom of a chronic virgin.

"I think we should do nine," Kira said.

"Didn't we do six last time?" Bron asked.

"Yes, but I think we have a pretty good handle at this point. We all know the difference between half a hit, one, two, three, five. We need to make a quantum jump. Tomorrow is going to be perfect."

Allen flipped the Suicidal Tendencies record he'd put on. "I agree," he said. "Nothing can go wrong out here. We know what we're doing."

"Okay," Bron said. "But if we're going for it, I want to be peaking at dawn. I've seen the sun rise too many times after tripping all night. This will be a totally new experience. Deal?"

Allen gave them both the thumbs up. Kira's right hand read, "I love you" in sign language. Bron made extra big Satan horns with both hands.

*

Thursday, June 19, 1986

The first alarm went off at 4:30am. At 5:02, the three unzipped their sleeping bags and started making breakfast. Quietly, they ate short stacks of buttery pancakes made from a bag of instant Krusteaz mix. Big glasses of pulpy Florida orange juice washed them down. Their stomachs would need this simple foundation to offset the acid. According to hearsay, the vitamin C was supposed to help them hallucinate harder.

Bron asked Allen, "Should we leave a note for your folks?"

"Nah. They don't care. I mean…they trust us. Not worried. Let's go."

Kira held the screen door open for the two young men then shut it softly behind them. No one on Blackberry Road ever locked their front door.

Outside, the morning was dark and very quiet. Once on the road, they walked the dashed yellow line westward down Blackberry toward Bellfountain. Their feet made the only sound, sneakers squeaking on blacktop. When they reached the corner, Kira sat on the low ledge of the concrete bridge. Starr Creek eddied and swirled six feet beneath them.

"Here, hold this will you?" Kira said.

She handed a small Maglite to Allen. Then she opened a film canister and unwrapped a clear plastic baggie. She started counting out hits, handing a strip to each of them. Bron popped one in his mouth.

Allen, still gripping the light, said, "Hey. This is ten, not nine."

"I know," Kira said. "I decided to upgrade us from coach to first class."

Bron shrugged and lifted his tongue. He wasn't too concerned about the difference between a nine-strip and a ten.

Allen succumbed and sucked his hits down. He tried to ignore the shudder that rushed up his spine the moment the paper contacted his flesh. His entire nervous system knew exactly what this meant. But physiological warnings are seldom heeded by teenage boys.

Kira whispered a Wiccan prayer, took the last of her own medicine.

They stopped at the next corner where a green road sign read Bellfountain one way and Starr Creek the other. A sodium vapor street lamp strobed high above the corner. Beyond that, asphalt shot straight into the darkness of western morn. A slight breeze rattled the telephone lines. Their choir of alien voices echoed down the road.

"There's no place like home," Allen said as he marched into darkness.

Three quarters of a mile down, the light at their backs grew as the world turned.

"It's all old houses and weird families if we keep going on the road," Allen said. "Let's head towards those fields to the right and catch the sunrise."

"I can feel something already," Bron said. "It's in my cheeks. Can't stop smiling."

"We took a lot," Kira said. "It's probably going to hit faster than usual."

The three strode off the road into waist-high grass. They hopped a weathered wood fence that seemed as much a part of nature as the tree line it guarded. Past those slender, leaning pines was Starr Creek. Its waters drifted ever eastward, deep and dark. Across both banks lay a felled tree bridge. The five feet of air between rounding bark path and cold black water below seemed to elongate as they crossed.

When they sat in a triangle in the center of the grassy field, the sun cracked across the eastern sky.

A psychedelic singularity overtook their minds.

Silence broke as the bees awoke.

Flowers opened like time-lapse video.

Shadows of trees coalesced and stretched.

Black sky grew blue and rose ever higher above.

The ground grew warm and dewdrops clung to pedals and blades.

Then Bron leaned forward and threw up.

"I'm making beer!" he said between spouts of regurgitated O.J.

He was fine, though. Bron's stomach often churned when drinking or drugging. The three just laughed and slapped him on the back and moved their magic circle a few feet to the left.

Waves of lysergic inebriation wafted in like heat shimmer tape warble. None of them could find words. They knew this was the time to buckle in like astronauts, endure the G's like an Olympic toboggan team.

Together they heard a ragged scream from across the field.

Kira looked wide-eyed at Bron who squinted at Allen who stared across the waving grass toward the sound. Wind whipped as six young eardrums contracted.

Things stayed quiet for so long that they began to believe they'd imagined it.

That's when the dog began to whimper.

From the same place across that wide field at dawn, they heard the sound of some poor hound being beaten senseless. Even the blows were audible despite the distance. Each wallop was followed by a dogged howl. Incessant, unrelenting. Blow, howl. Blow, howl.

Bron leaped to his feet. Kira grabbed his legs and pulled him back down. Allen was pressed to the ground, staying well below the level of the highest grass.

"What the actual fuck?" Bron said in a whisper. High as he was, the moment was mildly sobering.

"I don't know," Allen said. "But we are on private property. And everyone out here is armed."

Kira's face was unreadable. Her pupils kept dilating larger. The morning sun beat the trees' shadows into submission to the plaintive moans of a dying dog. After far too long, a single gunshot finally silenced those.

7

Puppy heard the cockcrow and looked upon the daybreak. When he turned his gaze back to Willie, ready to exact revenge, he saw only a tree stained with blood and a bungee cable lying on the ground. Then Puppy's feet pulled out from under him and his head hit the ground.

Hog-tied, Puppy could only get glimpses of Willie's bloodshot eye in its swollen socket. Each squirm led to another swift kick.

"Who's laughing now, Puppy dog?"

Puppy knew what a rhetorical question was, so he did not answer.

"Now, if you do the barking," Willie said, "I just might let you live."

The same boot had kicked Puppy out of the Golden Bough half a night, a gallon of gas, a pint of blood, and a squirt of piss earlier. Now it cracked against his ribs, which flexed underneath a dirty shirt soaked in cold sweat.

Puppy howled like a wounded dog. Anything to end this latest pain and humiliation. He wasn't proud. Another kick and he bayed at the sun like a wolf that missed its moon muse. Kick, howl. Kick, howl. He rolled in the dirt and cried.

Willie staggered in a circle, weak from blood loss, exhausted and stiff. He lifted the crowbar from the dirt, brought the bloody claw up near his eye and winced. Then he turned his gaze back to his quarry.

"Now, Puppy. We gonna see if dogs go to Heaven. Personally, I wouldn't bet on it."

Willie raised the bar above his head. Blue steel glinted in the diurnal radiance. There was the deafening report of a rifle. The crowbar clattered to the ground a second before Willie fell to his knees.

Puppy rolled over onto his back. His face was a swelling purple bruise. He half-smiled and moaned, then said, "Thanks, Kitty."

8

"Charles Leif, you run down to the store and pick me up my carton of Kings, pronto. You hear?"

He heard all right. His father never spoke in a quiet voice. Charles arose quickly for a boy his size. He silenced the *A-Team* re-run he'd been enjoying.

"Yes, Dad!" he said through the thin wall. "Come on, Ethan," he said to his friend.

They were classmates when school was in session. Friends on summer break. Charles only had one friend. If Ethan hadn't moved to the district at the start of the year, fifth grade would have been miserable. Ethan was the wiry teacher's pet; Charles learned more on the barren streets of Monroe than from any book he'd half-read.

The two boys left out the side door. The walk to the store was only a few blocks. Monroe was a tiny town. Ethan had his little AM radio with its single speaker cranked. They stomped like little giants down the center of the road, singing Eddy Grant. Fourth of July was only a few weeks off. Blowing up pretty much anything was highly appealing to their eleven-year-old egos.

Church Street finished after a few blocks. At Main, they cut left around the Boog. Across the highway leaned the junk shop. Both boys had spent rainy afternoons in there, flipping through crates of wrinkled ten-cent comics and sifting through drawers of arrowheads while the windowpanes rippled and dripped. The place was filthy, dim, and crowded with elk head taxidermy, smelly old wigs, and brass furniture scratched silver where the brass paint flecked off.

Charles gave the front door of Grieg's Market a push with his fat forearms. It flung open and smacked against a newspaper stand. Old man Grieg gave him the side-eye then went back to packing a glass milk bottle beside a two-liter missile of New Coke in a rasping plastic bag.

Some high school students were crowded around the arcade machine in the corner. The sounds of explosions and death rattles and melodramatic drama class voices bleeped from its speaker. Grieg had traded in the *Galaga* machine for *Gauntlet*. Ever since, Ethan and Charles had pretty much given up on playing. That machine served four at a time and had an insatiable hunger for quarters.

For a minute they stood on tiptoes and gazed between the bigger kids at the giant color screen. An elf maiden, a barbarian, and a wizard were losing badly against some deadly foe that was either invisible or off screen. The situation was not going well in those burning digital woodlands. The players were tense.

Ethan and Charles wandered away to huddle by the magazine rack. They both liked thumbing through the latest comics. A year earlier, they'd met right here. As Charles told the story, Ethan had made an impression by saying, "Move over, fatso." Ethan didn't remember it this way at all. He suspected that Charles made up the story to guilt him into friendship. It didn't really matter. Ethan liked Charles. So they were friends.

"Check it out, Ethan. This one's called Green Lantern's Corpse!"

Charles lifted a funny book with an array of different colored Green Lanterns on the cover. A giant pink-skinned alien hulked behind the rest.

"It says Corps, Charles. I think it's some kind of army thing. You know I quit buying comics when they jumped from sixty-five cents to seventy-five. So lame. It's only supposed to go up a nickel at a time. Anyway, let's check out the fireworks."

They meandered through the store over its cracked concrete floor past rows of dusty cans wrapped in fading labels. Meat counter smell permeated the place. The fireworks display stood tiered like a Mayan pyramid in a cubby at the far side. The pyrotechnic edifice overwhelmed them with its fiery reds, oranges, and yellows. It was all vastly out of their price range.

Ethan turned over a brick of Red Rats in his hand. "Wow, it's a gross," he said.

Charles looked at him funny. "They're still sealed. What's so gross?"

"No, I mean, there are 144 Red Rats in here," Ethan said without a hint of condescension. He held the brick like a crystal ball, as if peering at it hard enough would somehow make it his.

"Listen," Charles said. "I'll go distract the old man. You put that under your shirt and meet me in the brambles."

Before Ethan could react, Charles approached the counter and ordered a carton of his father's favorite brand. Ethan had never stolen anything. He felt his pulse double. He inched out of the shadow of the cubby toward the sunbeams streaming through the front door. It seemed like everyone was watching him. He had one hand under his shirt gripping the brick. The other was jammed low in his pants pocket unsure what to do with itself. He met his own eyes in the round mirror above the register and saw guilt in his distorted features.

Just then, the three bigger kids lost their *Gauntlet* game. They smacked the machine in disgust.

Old Grieg hollered, "Hey! I don't own those. I rent them. Treat it right or I can call the vendor. We can be back to pinball and *Space Invaders* inside of a week."

The kids just shook their heads and muttered complaints. They said things like, "My archer was kicking ass...too bad your pussy wizard ate that chest full of poison right when we got to the boss...how do you hit something you can't even see?"

Out front of the store, they donned cheap sunglasses and lit no-name cigarettes. Ethan had already disappeared around the corner.

Charles signed for his dad on the family tab. He left with a carton of Kings. He liked that his dad smoked those. Charles Leif patted himself on the back for having the last name of a Viking and the first name of a king.

He rounded the side lot of Grieg's and cut through the back alley toward the brambles. These were an unused block that had grown over with berry bushes and thistles. Someone had clipped paths for anyone willing to get their knees dirty. Candy wrappers and trash littered the ground. Charles didn't mind crawling but he loathed the thorns that scratched down his back. He was the same size around as those cramped burrows.

Deep in the center of the brambles, Ethan sat elated. He had already torn the brick apart and was counting out two piles of firecrackers to share. The boys huddled in the cave like pirates. Their voices mingled in minor cacophony with the calls of birds that preyed on the yellow jackets which also called the brambles home. Once the piles looked even, the boys scooped firecrackers into pants pockets and shirt pockets and underwear. Then they snuck out the backside of the brambles onto the street where Charles lived.

As they reached the carport beside the house, Jerry "Scary" Leif stepped out of the shadows. He snatched the cigarettes from Charles.

"What took you so long?" he said. It was a statement, not a question.

He gave Charles a little shove then wandered back to his Harley and stuffed the smokes in a saddlebag. The boys heard him kick start the bike which spit gravel when its back wheel spun. Then he was away. The tailpipe belched blue fumes, which echoed down the road with pure American flatulence.

9

Ethan and Charles had the house to themselves. They splashed whole milk over big bowls of sugar cereal. Matching *Knight Rider* TV trays stood before the old wood grain console television. They settled into deep cushions of the dusty, failing tweed couch, content to while away the rest of their day.

"That was pretty smooth back there. Nice job," Charles said, crunching a mouthful of Candy-O's.

Ethan blushed with pride. He knew that Charles was a bad influence. But each time Ethan skipped school or stood victorious after a dirt clod fight, he felt a bit more adult.

The show they were watching ended with Mr. T in a huff. The rest of the team laughed at him as white credits rolled over his thick gold necklaces and his shiny black face. A commercial came on: a motorcycle rounded a bent mountain road. But the sound of the bike was a narrator saying, "Rai...nier...Beeeeer." The boys chuckled as it ended. They looked forward to being older and riding motorcyles and drinking beer.

Then came a knock at the front door.

Charles picked up his bowl and slurped out the rest of the milk. Then he pushed his TV tray forward, rose, and walked to the door at his own slug pace. He could see one of the high school boys who had been hanging out in the market.

Through the torn screen door, the boy said, "Your dad around, chubby?"

"You see his hog in the driveway?" Charles asked. "I didn't think so. Buzz off."

"He was supposed to have something for me. You know what it is."

"Yeah. Come back later."

"I don't have time for that."

"I said no. Scram, Parker."

"Listen, I can't really 'come back later.' Tell you what. I'll throw in five bucks if you get it now."

"No way."

"Ten then."

Charles did the math. "All right. Hold on."

He didn't invite Parker in. Charles just left him standing outside the screen door shifting nervously. Parker seemed high-strung.

From down the shag carpet hallway, Ethan watched Charles head to the bathroom at the back of the house. Charles opened the medicine cabinet. He used his teeth to pry the lid off an amber plastic bottle and dumped a couple of round white pills into his palm. He put the bottle back and slammed the soap-spotted mirror. Charles ambled into the kitchen, tore some tin foil from an open drawer and scrunched it around the pills.

Parker got visibly excited when he saw the silver package in Charles' hand. He produced a ten-dollar bill from a leather wallet in his worn blue jeans. Then he counted out ten ones. Charles unhooked the latch, made the exchange. Neither said thank you. Parker took off and Charles headed toward the comfort of the fridge.

The kitchen was a mess. Stacks of old cookbooks slouched on the counter. A sticky plastic tablecloth was going orange from yellow. Charles put the stack of ones on the table and tugged his ten-spot taut. Then he held it up to the sunlight struggling to shine through the grease-glazed kitchen window. He didn't know what to look for, but he had seen someone on TV spot counterfeit bills some way like this.

Ethan brought the cereal bowls and dropped them in the sink. He saw the drawer with the tin foil left open. The roll was out of its box. He picked it up, punched the tabs on each end and fitted the foil back inside.

"See, check it out, Charles. If you punch in the tabs, it doesn't fall out of the box." Ethan smiled and closed the drawer.

"Where did you learn that, Betty Crocker?" Charles said with disdain.

"On *Mister Rogers*," Ethan said sheepishly.

"You're eleven. What are you doing watching *Mister Rogers*?"

"I don't anymore! I just remember the things that I see. You should try paying attention. You might get better grades, fatso," Ethan said. But he winked when he said it.

Charles almost took offense, then relaxed and smiled.

"So what are we going to spend the money on?" Ethan asked with a smirk. "Arrowheads? Fireworks? Green Lantern's Corpse?"

"Nah," said Charles. "I've got a better idea."

10

It took some time, but the gunshot eventually stopped echoing in their minds.

"Poor doggy," Kira said with a frown. She knew the dangers of letting spirits down with this much acid sprinting through their systems.

"Come on," she said. "Let's head for those hills." She pointed at a ridge to the south that was back toward Allen's home and far away from whatever backwoods madness they'd just witnessed at a distance.

All three crouched until they reached the tree line, anxious to avoid scrutiny. Once they were in the woods, the drug amplified, hitting harder. Each wondered if walking or standing was really an option but they just leaned into it and let momentum carry them. That is, until they reached the fallen tree over the creek.

For a few moments they all stood and stared at the

bridge and marveled at the coordination required to make such a crossing.

An eye blink later they stood on the far side. Their frying pan pupils said it all. None could imagine how they'd just crossed that log without falling in. It didn't make sense but it happened so fast. Time was like a rubber band and it had snapped them out of danger twice now. So they didn't argue and pressed on.

Over the fence, they crossed Starr Creek Road. There were no cars. No signs of people at all. Just crow calls in the distance and multi-acre squares of Christmas trees standing like green pawns on a sand and shadow chessboard. The trio wove between the boughs, enjoying the parallax of their vision as they passed each row of trees. The ground was caked with orange powder chemicals that kept indigenous insects from devouring some far off family's prefab holiday cheer.

Halfway up the ridge they stopped to huff and breathe. Kira passed her plastic gallon jug of water to Allen and Bron. They took long pulls and thanked her. The morning was still. Then they heard a rustle in the grass where the crop trees ended and wild forest began. Something they couldn't see blew by at high speed. It left only wind and parted grass in its wake.

"What the fuck was that?" Allen asked.

"Wendigo," Bron said. "Ridge-runner. Self cleaning."

They looked at each other and burst into laughter.

"Come on," Kira said. "Let's follow it." So they marched onward.

The trail through the trees was softer earth that saw far less sun than the caked, chemical-bleached dirt further behind. The ground was too dry for mud but felt squishy to their drugged feet like they were walking on the skin of a giant. Spears of sunlight lanced through the treetops, dotting the forest floor with dancing bright spots that slew the shadows they sliced.

Eventually the trees came to an end. The stony crest of the open ridge lay dead ahead. They followed it to its highest point and resumed their circle. They were still peaking on the most acid any of them had ever dared take at once. It was a relief to be at their destination. No one had fallen in the creek. No one had gotten shot by a crazy farmer whose dog had stolen a fresh pie from the window. That was what they agreed had happened. They'd all seen the scenario in countless cartoons and at that moment, everything was operating like a *Silly Symphony*.

From that height they saw quilt squares of valley below. Great leaden clouds spiraled closer round the ridge. A bank of fog shaped vaguely like a Viking ship crashed into them. For thirty seconds it rained sideways. Their faces were walloped with drops. Their hair blew back in the wind. Then the cloud ship's stern sailed by, leaving them stunned, standing to drip-dry in the warm mid-morning sun. This pattern continued for hours as they lingered and enjoyed the timeless cycling revolution of sun and fog. They were Oregonians after all. A little rain never hurt any one of them.

Bron had borrowed a crazy orange and silver ski jacket from Allen's parents' musty front hall closet. Now he put it on backwards, assumed the iconic warrior stance.

"I'm *Paranoid!*" he said.

"What's wrong now?" Kira asked.

"He's talking about the cover of a Black Sabbath album," Allen said.

42

Some basic snacks were stowed in one of the blousy pockets of Kira's army jacket. Allen was still laughing. He tore off a hunk of sourdough bread, which he chewed into glue. Bron abstained as his stomach was still settling.

Finally, the cloud ships crashed on the rocks, dissipating in the afternoon glare. The acidic tide was slowly going out again.

"Should we go back?" Bron asked.

"I don't really want to deal with my parents just yet," Allen said.

"What else is out here?" Kira asked. "We could try to find that guy's commune."

"I would have no idea where to look for that," Allen said. "There are so many properties out here and they all have No Trespassing signs planted out front."

Kira looked disappointed.

"But tell you what," Allen said. "Follow me, and I'll show you the Body Drop."

11

Puppy turned away from Kitty's enormous, blue-veined bosom as she untied his bonds. He'd seen his sister naked plenty of times and had no desire to ever again.

Once he was free he started on hands and knees. Then he rose slow, one paw propped on Kitty's shoulder. Her rifle was balanced on the wheeled walker she used to get around.

"How'd you find me," he asked.

"Well, you wasn't exactly quiet," she said. "But it was Babby as told me you was in trouble."

"Oh, you quit with that Babby talk, sis. You know well as I there ain't no such thing."

"So is! He watches my programs with me every morning. One time I set my hand right on his little head and he let me pet him."

"I've heard it before and I ain't likely to honor it now. You're crazier than a hog on ice but you're still my kin and

I love you for saving my skin. Guess we best head up to the Drop. Help me out with him. He's heavy as sin."

"Only if you quit rhymin'."

With great effort, Kitty heaved her pale frame over to Willie's cooling corpse. Puppy rolled the body into the tarp, which they wrapped and tied. Then each took a corner and started pulling.

Once they got him on gravel, the tarp pulled easier. Loose stones rolled below. Kitty wheezed for breath. Puppy's bruises smarted. But they were family and cleaning up messes was part of the deal.

What they didn't need was the rest of the camp to see what they were up to. Loose lips and all. As they dragged Willie past the old homestead, Puppy could see Squirrel through the wide-open front door. She was roosting in front of the boob tube, mutely hanging on Bob Barker's every word. The teen's wide eyes drank in the world but no human sound escaped her pretty mouth. She'd been schooled at the altar of the idiot box. Kitty also read passages to her from the great black book that Ma Tyler passed down. Squirrel rocked like there was a breeze in the house and she was a dandelion anxious to become someone's wind drifting wish.

Kitty stopped with a gasp. She held a slender hand over her bacon-wrapped heart. 'Egg-on-stilts' the cruel country school children had called her. So she came home and let Ma teach her the old ways instead. Her hand sank into the lichen that grew on the side of the house. Moss draped off stolen dish antennae, all corroded and aimed at teasing satellites and irritable sunspots and often nothing but the silent void of space.

"C'mon," Puppy said. "Almost there."

They resumed the literal drag, pulling Willie into a cluster of tall grass and ferns that obscured the tunnel entrance. The wood frame enclosing the portal gave it the look of a bunker or mineshaft. This network of passages was a remnant of the feud their family had won. It connected all points of the property. The siblings hoisted their cargo into a cart. Puppy ran back to fetch Kitty's walker and her rifle. She took a seat on one end of the rickety tumbrel. Then he rolled them both into the darkness.

12

"Voila," Allen said. "The Body Drop."

Kira and Bron stood with arms folded.

"It's a cistern," said Bron.

"Maybe," Allen replied. "But you've never seen one this deep. Check it out."

In a small clearing angled just where the sun wouldn't touch it there was a round metal hatch dead center in the ground. Allen threw the bolt. It squeaked open on dirt-caked stainless hinges. A hollow wind escaped the shaft. Allen's skateboard side-bangs fluttered loosely over his wire rims.

Bron leaned down and whistled. The echo seemed to drown down the endless distance. Kira dropped in a pebble, listening for any sound, hearing none at all.

"Wow," she said. "This would be an excellent place to drop a body. Any volunteers?" She smirked.

Satisfied that Allen was not full of shit and that he'd

shown them a wonder worthy of their trip, they closed the hatch and wandered back into the trees. They were barely three deep in the phalanx of firs when the creak and commotion of Puppy pushing his cart out of the woods and into the clearing caught their ears. All three teens dropped to silent knees and watched.

"You don't think she'd want him?" Puppy asked.

"The old Goat has no liking for dead flesh," Kitty answered. "She prefers virgins, which is why we're both still here. I reckon we'd have been offered up long ago if you wasn't such a curious bugger when we was kids."

Puppy shuddered at the memory and locked the wheels of the cart.

"I got this," he said.

He opened the hatch in the ground and tipped the cart sideways. The great tarp-wrapped lump flopped over into the hole. One end smacked the rim on its way then disappeared in descent toward the core. Puppy slammed the hatch shut, turned his purple face to the sky and sighed.

"Glad that's done," he said. "I need a bath and some balm."

Kitty shouldered her rifle, leaned on her walker. She curled her lips in a smile over her double-rowed jumble of teeth.

"Good boy, Puppy," she said with genuine affection.

They had just turned to wheel the cart back into the trees when Allen shifted his weight from his sleeping foot. A twig snapped in the maddening silence. Bron's jaw dropped and Kira's eyes widened in horror. They saw Puppy cast the cart aside and whirl around. Kitty unslung her gun and cocked it, surveying the low treetops in their general direction. It would not take long for them to find their spies.

Kira knew there was little time and acted. She made a hand motion that meant *trust me* to the boys. Then she proceeded to stand and waltz into the clearing.

Allen and Bron kept an eye on her while they quietly backed further into the trees.

"Why you creeping, girl?" Puppy shouted at Kira as he strode toward her. "What did you see?"

Kira stood her ground. Her résumé as Trip Captain had prepared her for being Zen in the worst moments.

"See? I didn't see anything. But some animal did blow past me in a hurry. I followed it and got lost. Can you please point me to the road? I'm afraid I'm going to get poison oak up here if I don't get back on a good trail."

"Where'd you come from?" Kitty asked her.

"I'm just visiting my aunt for the summer. I live out by the wildlife preserve," Kira lied.

She hoped she sounded believable but found it hard to gauge anything with the afterglow of ten hits in her system.

"So," she said. "Could you, like, please show me the way out of here?"

"Not likely," Kitty said. Then she staggered forward and shoved Kira to the ground and aimed the rifle between her eyes.

Puppy opened the hatch again.

Kira gulped and realized that she was sacrificing herself in order to save her friends. Of a sudden, it seemed a foolish move. Her hands were sweating and all she could think to do was whisper a protection charm under her breath that she'd overheard from her mother's coven.

Bron and Allen were quietly losing their minds in the trees, terrified for their friend and themselves. They

49

were just about to run out into the clearing with no plan whatsoever when the familiar sound of a Volkswagen engine came growling up from the road below.

Everyone froze in place and strained to see the vehicle. The driver's door opened and out strode a man. He was lean, toned, and widow's peaked. He marched up the path with one hand perched on a holster at his belt.

While he ascended the ridge, no one moved or spoke. It would have been comical if the Drop weren't so deep. Soon enough, he was in their midst.

"Afternoon, Rex," Puppy said.

Kitty squinted and spat.

"Afternoon. What exactly are you two up to?" Rex asked.

"Little bitch was spying on us," Kitty said. "And trespassing."

"Was not!" Kira exclaimed. "I'm just lost. Help me find the road, mister?"

Rex reached a hand out to her, pulled her behind him.

"Last time I checked, this wasn't your property, Kitty. Neither is the girl. Let's go on and forget all about this. I'm sure she's done you no harm. Alright, neighbors?"

Allen and Bron were inching their way further from the scene. Allen could see that Puppy had finally noticed them. His gaze was burning as he memorized the boys' features.

Kitty just stood there, holding her gun, chewing her lip, saying nothing.

Rex turned his back on them and gently pushed Kira down the path toward his bus. At the foot of the ridge she stepped onto the sunbaked snakeskin of the road and climbed into the vehicle. Rex put it in gear and drove east, deeper down Starr Creek and away from Allen's farm.

13

Kira strapped on the lap belt. She'd already figured out the weird German mechanism during her first ride on this particular bus. Rex downshifted from third. The tall knobbed stick shuddered between the seats for a second as they clunked from pavement down to gravel. He seemed highly distracted and kept glancing in the rear view mirror. Finally, Kira had to break the silence.

"Thanks again. I hope my friends made it out of there."

Rex slammed on the brakes. They slid to a halt on the rocky road.

"Friends? I didn't see them! Why didn't you say something?"

"They were hiding. I don't know. Hopefully they snuck off while we were all talking."

"Well," he said. And then he left it at that and put the van back in gear. They started moving again.

"Those are some really dangerous people," he said. "I try to get along with them since we share the road. Neighbors have to look out for each other around here. But we better make sure they don't see you again."

"I never planned to get in the way." She gazed out the window at the passing foliage. "I have something else to confess to you, Rex."

"You can tell me anything, Kira. You know I'm safe. I got you to your friend's house last night. And I put myself between you and the Tylers today. What's on your mind?"

"I'm tripping right now. Really heavily. I have been all morning. I do LSD pretty much every weekend. Only right now, it's summer vacation. So every day is the weekend."

"Ha! That's your confession? Well little lady. You are coming to the right place."

He smiled, then put his hand over her eyes and cranked the wheel hard to the right.

She was too startled to push him away. She just gripped the seat and made sure not to smack her head on the window or dash. When he finally put his hand back on the wheel they were driving through a heavily forested mud track that seemed like a logging road. It twisted and forked several times. Rex seemed to pick paths that were purposely confusing. There was no way she could have retraced her way out or drawn a map of the road. Even sober she'd have relied on the sun or the stars over her convoluted memory.

The shade ended and the bus came puttering out onto a long straight path that was really just two wheel ruts the width of the VW's tires. Rolling green hills of unkempt tall grass waved in either direction. They crossed the last rise and descended into a vale that was dotted with what looked like giant golf balls half-submerged into the soil circuiting a large pond, or maybe a small lake. Kira knew what she was looking at though. Geodesic domes.

"The commune!" she exclaimed with delight.

"Yes, indeed. Welcome to Nemi."

Once they'd parked, Rex let Kira out then opened the back hatch. Several men with cowled faces approached and began silently unloading the parcels stacked inside. Their eyes regarded Kira but she could not decipher their judgment.

Rex led her toward a grove by the lake. Two women with assault rifles seemed to be on guard. When Rex made a simple gesture they bowed their heads and stood aside. There was a tall tree in the center. Rex gave it a wide berth. He led Kira toward a bench on the other side that faced the lake and offered her a seat.

One of the guardians brought them a bottle of wine, uncorked it, and poured. Then Rex dismissed her. He handed a full glass to Kira.

"I don't drink," she responded out of habit.

The whole situation was truly overwhelming. Her senses were already maxed out from the morning, her surroundings, the mysteries of Rex and Nemi, and her concern for Allen and Bron.

Rex laughed aloud. "You're on acid at this very moment, but you don't drink?" He smiled.

Kira couldn't help but laugh in return. Rex's calmness did help distract her mind from its various stresses.

"What if I told you," he asked, "that this is sparkling cider?"

She sniffed it. Tasted it. Golden and delicious and

sparkling like the sunlight on the lake water before her.

He clinked his glass against hers and took a sip of his own.

"We call this lake Diana's Mirror."

Kira's wrist went limp and she almost dropped her glass. Dianic Wicca was what her mother practiced.

"Yes," he said. "I see you already knew. This doesn't surprise me. You're a special young lady, Kira. I don't think our meeting was purely by chance. Do you?"

Kira wasn't sure how to respond. So she took another drink. Was it cider or wine? The acid made her taste buds explode like rainbows were crash landing on them. Suggestion was such a powerful thing. She felt lightheaded. Experience taught her that standing and walking cleared her mind. So she stood and walked toward the water. Rex's gaze followed her.

At the lake's edge she set down her glass and kicked off her shoes. In one motion, she pulled her shirt and jacket off and walked into the water. It felt warm and reflected sky and sun in cerulean blue and honey gold. Her arms parted, stroked, and carried her out into its center. Concentric circles rippled outward and dissipated into the great comforting stillness of the water.

14

Allen and Bron were sprinting through the trees as fast as their drug-addled legs would carry them. One moment Puppy was a few yards behind them. The next he'd disappeared. They just kept going and the fence between them and Bellfountain Road kept getting larger and closer. Then without warning a canvas flap the color of dirt burst open and out sprang Puppy from a hole in the ground. He was so close that it seemed pointless to run. Bron whirled around, flipped open the butterfly knife that he kept on his belt and swung it right in Puppy's face. Allen just kept on sprinting.

Puppy looked at the little blade and smiled. There was a thin red line on his cheek where Bron had drawn blood. He touched it with a finger, tasted it. In one smooth motion he swept Bron's legs out from under, took the knife, and pinned him to the ground. Blade to throat, Bron could smell vomit and dog food and hate on Puppy's breath. Before he could mentally cork it, Bron's bladder let loose.

There was a second or two of staring eye to eye that seemed like hours. Then both heard the blip of a police siren and Bron saw red and blue lights reflected in Puppy's bloodshot eyes. Puppy kept the knife pinned to the boy's jugular and turned his gaze up toward Allen who had nearly reached the road. A county sheriff had just pulled over a carload of what looked like migrant farm workers packed into a tiny hatchback. Now Allen was climbing over the fence and waving his arms. Puppy growled in frustration. After another moment of indecision, he spat in Bron's face and disappeared back into the hole. Once he was in, Bron found it hard to see where the opening even was.

Allen looked back and saw his friend standing alive and alone amongst the trees. The two met at the corner and tried to stroll away from Starr Creek casually. That was no mean feat considering the excessive drugs and the giant piss stain on Bron's jeans. Still they managed to walk back to Allen's farm without any more scrutiny. The cop simply raised an eyebrow at them and resumed hassling his innocent victims.

*

Inside the ranch house Allen's mother was watching TV. Bron excused himself to take a shower and change. Under the hot rain, the acid surged. The ceramic tub seemed too slick to stand on, so he sat. Eventually, when he felt a semblance of normalcy, he shut down the jets and toweled off. He took a comb to his long black hair and stared into the mirror at his enormous pupils. That was just about enough alone time he decided. So he unhooked the latch to rejoin the family.

Allen's mom beckoned for him to take a seat. She and her son were sharing the couch. Allen's dad was presumably at work on a Wednesday afternoon. That left the La-Z-Boy for Bron, which suited him just fine. He grabbed the side lever and yanked the padded footrest into position. Just then, a commercial came on, and Lillian Easley got up.

"You boys sure got an early start today. You must be starving by now. I'll whip something up for you," she said with a smile. Then she headed into the kitchen and opened the freezer door.

"Where did Kira take off to?" Lillian wondered aloud.

Bron and Allen exchanged looks that rode the border between confusion and guilt. Finally Allen answered, "She caught a ride to Philomath with a friend. I think she'll be back a little later."

He shrugged at Bron, hoping that he didn't sound insane. It seemed to satisfy his mother, though. She just popped something in the oven and wound the mechanical timer into position.

When Lillian sat back down, the commercial break was over and the show was resuming. She re-immersed herself in an episode of *Magnum P.I.*, the one where Magnum falls off a boat into shark-infested sea. He has to tread water for twenty-four hours in order to survive.

Lillian thought Tom Selleck was hot. Bron and Allen were much more focused on keeping their heads above water. On all that acid, they found it hard to breathe while watching the show. It seemed to go on forever.

Magnum had one flashback after another of being abusively forced to learn to swim as a boy. Finally, a rope ladder dipped into the ocean and Magnum was rescued. The boys sighed with relief. They took deep breaths. Their heart rates slowed. The timer in the kitchen began to ding and the smell of Tyson chicken nuggets emanated throughout the house. Eating those would be their next trial.

15

Puppy crawled out of the hole closest to home. By the time he got to the entrance to the tunnel with the tracks he could just hear Kitty's curses and see the wobbling beam of her light aching its way out. He nearly took his head start as a blessing then thought better. His face was bleeding and he hadn't eaten human food in three days. He felt dirty even for him. And he was dog-tired. But his sister had just plucked his bacon from the frying pan mere hours before. She deserved his shoulder to lean on.

Though her weight was not inconsiderable, Puppy used the last of his strength to get her inside the main house. He plunked her down on an immense, mold-ringed sofa that had long since collapsed yet received no mercy now.

"Squirrel!" she called out. "Draw Puppy a bath. He stinks to pits. And he's hurting too."

The girl jumped at the sound of her name and fled the room on her errand in an instant.

Puppy scavenged around the kitchen. He found a turkey leg to gnaw on while he cranked a can of beans into an old skillet over a butane flame. Once the pile of pintos uncongealed, he cracked a can of Stroh's and stumbled back down to the den. The whole place was filled with detritus and memorabilia from a hundred ransacked mobile homes and abandoned cabins. Beams were nailed up at odd angles just to keep the rain off but the warm afternoon wind whistled through a dozen weak points.

Kitty flipped through the channels as if they didn't roll over again at zero. She landed when Dick Hyman's theme for *Search For Tomorrow* played. Instinctively, she reached a hand out to Babby since *Search* was one of her special programs. Her nails just clawed at open space. When Puppy limped into the room with a plate of steaming beans, she snatched her hand back and blushed.

"Can't believe you let them kids get away," she said, to distract him.

Puppy didn't respond. He just plopped down beside her to stare at the TV and shovel beans to fill the hole in his gut. On screen, a woman in a violet dress with enormous shoulder pads was imploring a tan man with bleach blonde hair that 'theirs was a special love that the world would never understand.' Puppy glanced over at Kitty. She was using the giant remote control to itch between two folds of her gut fat. He inched away from her a little and set his plate down on the chipping walnut armrest.

Squirrel whisked back into the room and pulled at his arm.

"Hold your horses. I'm coming," he said. He got up slow and felt every muscle twinge and spasm. His bruises had bruises at this point.

"I'll catch up with them kids," he said to Kitty before he

left. "I got a real good look at the big one. Even caught a souvenir," he said. Then he flipped open the butterfly knife for effect.

Kitty was absently staring at the screen and took no notice. Puppy stuck the blade in the arm of the couch by his cooling plate and stormed out of the room. When he was gone, Kitty reached for the plate and started finishing it for him. When she was sure no one was watching, she licked Puppy's blood off the knife tip too.

The bath was a splash of heaven on earth. Usually the creek was plenty good enough for him to get wet and tame his scent. But all the fear and pain, exhaustion and rage had caught up with him. Steam danced on top of the water, a little orgy of hot devils squaredancing to a fiddle on fire. Puppy settled in, tried to mentally unknot each corded muscle. He closed his eyes.

Squirrel watched him for a time. He looked so peaceful. Such a rare moment of weakness. She wondered if she could slit his throat and get out of there for good. When she'd first run away and found the camp, he was kind to her a few times. Kitty and the others yelled and smacked and tried to find her voice. But there wasn't one to find and Puppy was ok with that. So she started being kind to him back. But soon his actions told the same story all over again. She knew how to be kind to a man and it never lasted. They always turned cruel. Puppy was bad or worse than any of them.

Soon he started to snore. His lips flapped bubbles in the tub and still he slept. Squirrel reached a slight hand toward his throat. Carefully, quietly. She knelt beside the tub with a wicked kitchen knife gripped tight in her other hand below the rim of the tub. If she could just pin him, steal his air…closer…closer…

Puppy's eyes shot open and snatched her reaching hand by the wrist and twisted. Squirrel gasped, which was only an intake of breath and dropped the blade in fright. Just as quick, she snatched up the jar of balm and raised it toward his face.

"That's what I thought," he said and released her.

She used her free hand to dip a finger in the viscous liquid and smear a thick line of it across Puppy's good cheek—the one with the long thin knife slice. The other side of his face was getting darker as the day went on. She went to fetch a thin slice of deer meet to drape over that one. Puppy watched her go and remembered when she used to give it up without a fight.

From the tub, he could just reach the top of the toilet where his magazines were stacked. He fumbled open the tri-panel in the middle of the one on top and went to work on himself. When Squirrel walked back in the room she saw what he was about and fled in disgust. That did it for him. He flung the magazine to the floor and splashed his spunk to where it wouldn't cling to his skin.

Finally he climbed out and dried off with a shredded towel that hung off a bent nail in the wall. Wrapped in only that, he trudged into the den.

"I'm for bed. Nobody wake me for nothing. I plan to sleep on through 'til tomorrow."

"And what about those boys?" Kitty asked.

"Fools like those always come back for seconds," he said. "Anyway, I got an errand to run in the morning. You need anything from town, you tell me then. That goes for you too, Squirrel. No notes, now. You want something, you can whisper it in my ear."

16

Kira swam back the same way she came, like a reflection. She walked out of the water, dripping dry in the heat as the sun sank across the sky toward the horizon.

Rex stood, his boots sinking into the soft soil. Kira approached him. She felt dazed, drunk. Refreshed by the water, overwhelmed by the view of the grove and Rex standing before his sacred place. He had a power and a calm that she had never encountered before. As a psychonaut and explorer, she craved a deeper understanding, total immersion. She took his hand and placed it on the soggy bra that stuck to her left breast.

"How old are you?" Rex asked.

"Fifteen," she said.

"That's what I thought. Put your shirt on," he said, and walked a few paces to retrieve it. He handed it to her.

The oddest part to her was not the rejection. But the

strange lack of feeling when he touched her. She'd expected something electric. Instead, there was nothing.

"We have a lot to discuss, Kira. How did the water make you feel?"

"Very calm," she said, with honesty.

"Good. I need you to focus on what I have to say. There is something that's lived in these woods for a long time. It is fast. It is deadly. And it has never allowed itself to been seen."

"I know," she said. "I saw it today."

"You what?" Rex seemed alarmed for the first time since they'd reached Nemi.

"Well, I mean I didn't actually *see* it. But something shot by us at high speed. We followed it for a while. But then those awful people headed us off."

Rex was impressed. "I'm glad I don't have to convince you, then. Because whatever it is, it is here. And it is real. For many years it has aided some families and torn others apart. There seems not rhyme or reason to its whims. But all who live here fear it. It has many names…"

"Bron called it a Wendigo."

Rex laughed. "That one is new to me. But good as any. Something tells me, Kira, that you are the one who can help us find it. It has eluded me for decades."

Kira wondered at that. Sure, Rex's hairline had receded a little. She wasn't the greatest judge of age. And she was still coasting down off ten hits of acid. But even when she'd met him the day before, she didn't peg him as being older than maybe twenty. Clearly he was being dramatic.

"How can I help?" she asked. "I already told you that I couldn't really see it even when it passed right in front of me—if there was anything even really there at all. We were tripping hard. It wouldn't be the first mutual group hallucination I've shared with those dorks."

"Kira. Recall when I told you that you had come to the right place? I have a substance here that will blow your mind as it opens your senses. It is the third eye."

"Why don't you try it?" she asked.

"Oh, I have. Unfortunately its properties don't work for me. Not to the extent that I need. Kira, I want you to be my eyes. Will you do this for me?"

In the last twenty-four hours Rex had picked her up on the side of the road without being remotely creepy. Then he had saved her from being shot and thrown into a bottomless pit by insane hillbillies. And he'd declined his chance to take advantage when she was feeling weak.

"Yes, Rex. If I can see what you can't, I'll be happy to show you. But it can't be tonight. I'm too high already."

"Of course!" He seemed overjoyed. "Please stay with us tonight. I want you to enjoy the safety of Nemi.

"Well, I do need to let my friends know I'm OK. And my mom, at some point."

"Yes, but that will have to wait 'til tomorrow, I'm afraid. The Tylers will be watching. It's not safe yet. Can you be patient?" He raised the wine bottle, tilted his head and smiled.

"Yes," she said. "I can be very patient."

She dined with Rex that night and they spoke for hours. When her eyelids began to droop, he escorted her to a bunkhouse where many women slept and bid her good-night.

Kira closed her eyes but felt those of another upon her.

The next cot over, a young woman was watching. Kira peered toward her.

"What is it?" she asked.

"Are you the one who sees? Rex Neverending tells us that you are."

"I guess so," Kira answered. "Why do you call him never ending?"

"Because. He is the ageless one. He was first here. We all came to be with him."

"Why did you come?"

"This world is killing itself. It has turned its back on life and hope. Rex promised us freedom and passage to another world."

"And you believe him?"

"Of course. He cares for us all."

"Is it a good life here?"

"Yes! But it is not safe to leave Nemi. Nowhere else is safe. Will you stay with us?

"No," Kira said.

"Will you return, then?"

"We shall see."

17

"You know what to say in the morning, right?" Charles asked Ethan.

"Yeah. My folks know I'm here all weekend. But I'll tell yours that you're staying with us."

"Perfect."

They were both in sleeping bags, spooning head to foot in Charles' bed. Ethan tried to keep from rolling toward his friend since the mattress tended to sink that direction. But they were eleven and didn't care all that much.

After the lights had been out for a while, Charles nudged Ethan and waved a beaming flashlight in his eyes. Ethan winced at the brightness then took hold of the silver shaft with its red plastic fixtures. Charles handed him a magazine rolled up with a thick rubber band.

Ethan had examined a few issues of Playboy that his parents had left around. And he'd seen *Porky's* at the drive-in. But nothing quite like this. Pages and centerfolds in full color. Naked women not just posing, but in lurid action. One issue even featured Ozzy Osbourne dressed as a magician or maybe a vampire. A nude girl was kneeling on a pool table and Ozzy was using the crack of her ass to guide a pool cue toward a winning shot. Ethan was dumbfounded and aroused.

"Can I have one of these?" he asked Charles.

"Tell you what. Come with me to get more tomorrow and I'll give you the whole stack."

"Deal."

After a while, Ethan clicked off the flashlight. But sleep did not come quickly.

Friday, June 20, 1986

In the morning, Ethan rose late. Charles was already up. Loud voices and commotion echoed from the kitchen. Ethan dressed in yesterday's clothes and stumbled out to see what was going on. When he opened the bedroom door, he was greeted with the smell of Eggo waffles and Sizzlean.

"Morning, Ethan," said Charles' mother Jackie. She was a lot nicer than Jerry.

"Good morning, Mrs. Leif."

Ethan sat down and poured a glass of Tang.

"I don't want you two getting into trouble after we split," Jerry said, chewing his meat with an open mouth. "When are your folks coming?"

"They're picking us up at noon," Ethan lied. "I told them Charles was staying with us 'til Sunday night. If that's okay?"

"It better be. We don't have room for him on the bike," Jerry said. He turned to look at his son. "Country Fair starts tomorrow, Charles. We're due at Minnie's to pre-game."

"Jerry Leif!" Jackie snapped.

He cleared his throat. "I meant to say. We're going to cheer up Aunt Minnie. Uncle Willie done run off again. Ethan?" He turned to the other boy. "Make sure Charles doesn't clean out your fridge. He has some bad habits."

Charles gritted his teeth, embarrassed. But he was used to this sort of treatment.

"I won't pig out, Dad. Ethan's parents are real nice. They always have good stuff over there for me."

"Great. Saves me money."

*

After they finished, all the dirty dishes were stacked in the sink and forgotten. Ethan and Charles hid out in the bedroom while Jerry and Jackie stuffed saddlebags and knapsacks full of supplies for a weekend of hard partying. Finally they climbed on the Harley, cranked some Zeppelin on the bike stereo and waved goodbye. Ethan wondered if Jerry had trouble steering with a woman twice his size on the back. But they seemed to manage fine. And soon they were out of sight.

"Four days of freedom!" Charles exclaimed. He laid out his palm for a 'gimme five.' Ethan smiled and slapped it.

"So," Ethan said, "where do we get you some new magazines?"

"Up in Bellfountain," Charles answered. "It's all set up for one-thirty this afternoon."

"How are we going to get over there? That's miles away."

"That's the fun part. C'mon."

Charles led Ethan into the carport and to the shed at the back. There was a hefty padlock on the door. Charles produced a key, snapped the lock open and swung the door wide. Inside were two Honda ATC three-wheelers, shimmering in the fumes of a full can of gas.

18

By the time Bron noticed the scratching on Allen's bedroom window, morning was upon them. His plan had certainly worked. Tripping at dawn meant the young men actually got a good night's sleep afterward. That was something completely different.

He sat up in his sleeping bag and rubbed the sleep out of his eyes. Then, through the fog of post-psychedelic hangover, he remembered the events of yesterday. He recalled the look Puppy had given him while studying his face. Bron slowly gave the blinds a quarter turn and saw Kira waving at him with a smile. Then she put a finger to her lips and made a key-turning motion. He took the hint and padded silently through Allen's house. Half his blood was native; he took pride that Allen, not he, had cracked the twig.

Normally the front door was never locked at this house

but Bron had taken it upon himself to add a layer of protection overnight. Just in case Puppy came prowling. The last thing he wanted to do was invite danger upon Allen's innocent family.

Kira practically jumped through the front door and gave him a gigantic hug. Bron hugged her right back, elated and relieved that she was okay.

"How's life on the commune?" he whispered.

She smiled. "Better than you think. I brought back some mementos."

"You can tell us the whole story once we wake up Allen."

"Okay," she said. "Let's do that now. Because I really need to get home before my mom freaks out. Tell you both the whole story on the drive."

*

"I get it," Bron said. "You've got a crush on the guy. That's cool. I didn't even know you liked guys."

Kira punch him in the arm. Hard. The car swerved, but only a little.

"Hey," Allen cried from the back seat. "No attacking the driver. Until after we get out of the car."

Bron drove on with his hurt arm and massaged it with his good one.

"I forget about that right hook," he said. "Anyway, tell me more about the doses."

"Well, the way Rex described it, it's acid. Only it's not. That is, it has other properties. Sight beyond sight."

"Thunder, thunder, Thundercats! Ho!" Allen said, giggling in the back seat.

Kira didn't know what he was talking about so she ignored him.

"Well," asked Bron, "is it acid or not?"

"He called it Resonator. It's a liquid. I got a few drops. He said it doesn't take much but he might not know how seasoned we are. I tried to tell him."

"When do you want to try it?" Bron asked.

"Saturday," she said. "You know, if we do it two days in a row, it's just not the same. Our systems need a day to recalibrate."

They all nodded. Based on their mutual experiences, she was right.

Bron cranked up the stereo for the rest of the drive into town.

19

"Don't we need helmets?" Ethan asked.

"Yeah, I was thinking about that," Charles answered. "Check this out." He went back in the house. There was the sound of a bedroom closet door slamming open on rollers then plastic crashing on plastic. Charles returned with two matching green helmets. Both bore clear plastic visors and were attached to black ray guns on spiral cords.

"Photon!" Ethan said with excitement.

He remembered being really jealous when Charles got the set last winter. Ethan's parents celebrated Hanukkah, not Christmas. Nobody in the history of the world had gotten laser tag for Hanukkah. Charles' parents weren't known for their generosity but Jerry Leif saw Photon as a gateway to teaching his boy how to pull a trigger and hit a moving target. Win-win. Though he probably would have been pissed to find out that on this day the helmets were getting priority over the guns.

Ethan and Charles wheeled the ATCs out into the yard. Charles went back inside to close the curtains. He locked up the house and the shed. Each boy suited up with his turtle-green headpiece and attached the gun holster to his blue Cub Scout belt.

These trikes were nearly new Hondas. They fired up at the turn of a key, engines purring smoothly. There was no such thing as an American three-wheeler, which explained why the Leifs kept them locked up out of sight. It wouldn't do for anyone in Jerry's gang to catch wind of his transgression.

The boys pulled the clutch levers, toed their machines into gear and headed for the hills. Midday sun beamed straight down; they seemed to cast no shadow. The only danger was to the insects that died on the visors of their Photon helmets.

Charles led the way. Where there were clear roads, they boldly cruised on pavement. And when there were shortcuts through open fields, they took those. Sometimes they caught air, jumping over ruts and mounds. Otherwise they aimed for speed. Families of pheasants scattered as they passed. Farmers waved or shooed them on to other pastures. When the going was smooth they took their laser guns from their holsters and blasted thin air in triumph.

Bellfountain was a tiny dot on the map. An old white schoolhouse sat across the road from an erect finger of a church with round black windows. And down at the crossroads stood a lone phone booth that still cost a dime. Beside it was a country market with dueling gas pumps out front. Towns didn't come more rustic or quaint. The population sign read "23."

Charles led Ethan to the gas pump for a fill-up.

"Just to be on the safe side. These things don't have the greatest range," Charles said.

He unscrewed the gas cap and looked inside. The fuel looked as full as when they'd left.

"Never mind," he said sheepishly. "Anyway, *I'm* low on fuel. You hungry?"

He screwed the cap back on, removed his Photon gear and entered the little store. Ethan was right behind him.

This place was even smaller and dingier than Grieg's. And there were no arcade games at all. It felt like they had traveled back in time to when everything sucked. Charles led them to the cooler to pick out drinks and a couple of foot-long hot dogs. The woman at the register took his money and put the dogs in a slowly rotating radar range. Ethan could see hot air bursting the plastic bubble around his lunch like a blimp. When the oven bell chimed he popped open the bag and started scarfing. The warm scent of processed meat overtook the place. Charles was loading his up with a variety of condiments—one of everything the nice lady had on hand. To stave the mess, Charles took a big wad of napkins with him. He nodded at the lady and headed back outside. Ethan squeaked out a "thanks" for them both as the door swung shut.

They took a moment to finish their drinks in the early afternoon sun. Then Charles sent Ethan back inside to collect the deposits on the bottles. Ethan returned a minute later with four pieces of Bazooka bubble gum to cleanse their palates. They liked to read the little comics the gum came wrapped in.

Ethan's comic showed a boy in a long red turtleneck

with a ball of black yarn in his hand.

"This is enough for 3 socks?" the boy in the sweater asked his one-eyed friend Joe.

"3 socks?" Joe asked.

"My mom wants to knit socks for my brother in the army!"

"Why 3 socks?"

"He wrote in his letter—'2 weeks in the army and I've grown *another foot!*'"

The final frame was an ad for X-ray glasses with a mailing address in St. Paul, Minn.

Ethan put the comic carefully into his Velcro wallet. He had always wanted some X-ray glasses.

"The better to see you with," he said under his breath.

20

Bron and Allen dropped Kira in her driveway and made a date to call her in the evening to make a plan. She waved and marched up the stoop of a nondescript suburban home with a manicured lawn. The only ornamentation was a tinkling wind chime on the porch and a stained glass crescent moon built into the front door.

The Dart cruised down King's Blvd in Corvallis past the Bob's Burgers.

"Do you need to get home too?" Allen asked.

"Nah. A phone call will do. As long as my parents know I'm with you, they don't worry."

"What gave them that false sense of security?" Allen said with a laugh.

"Good question. Where to next?"

"Dude, it's Friday. I haven't checked on my subscriptions this week. Can we swing by Hagar's?"

Two minutes later, they pulled into a spot around the corner from the comic shop.

Bron didn't have money to browse so he just hung close to Allen. Hagar was behind the counter. He was always behind the counter or the place wasn't open, because he didn't trust anyone. While he was fetching Allen's subscriptions from a file, he kept glancing over the boys' shoulders toward the back of the room.

"Here we are, Mr. Easley. Just these two, I'm afraid. *Dark Knight 4* seems to be back ordered." Allen handed over his money. "And you, in the back," Hagar cried across the store, "I do hope you're planning to buy something."

Allen and Bron craned their necks to see the shabby character rifling through the porn section. They knew not to go back there because Hagar never let anyone under eighteen in that area for fear of a boycott by neighborhood parents. The guy in the back had a few adult magazines bundled with some old pulps from the twenty-five cent bin. He turned to give Hagar a withering look, then spotted Allen and Bron. His red-rimmed eyes and blotched and bruised face broke into a canine smile.

Puppy started walking toward the register with the mags in one hand and cash in the other. By the time he dropped the fluttering bills and a fistful of clattering change on the counter, Allen and Bron were already out the door and around the corner. They hopped through the open windows of the Dart like Duke boys and peeled out just as Puppy rounded the bend. He stood in place, memorizing the car, the license plate, the scent.

Only a day had passed and the hellhound had already found their trail.

21

Bron floored the Dart. Allen knelt in the back seat watching for any sign that they were being chased. Before long he saw the pickup truck.

"He spotted us!"

Bron took a sharp left, tires screeching around the corner. The car was so long, there was constant danger of hitting parked cars on the little side streets. So he blew the next stop sign and headed for a wider road. As they screamed on by, a kid had to jump off his skateboard and belly flop in the grass to keep from getting creamed. They maintained their lead but Puppy wasn't easily shaken. The truck's engine was no match for the Dart's but this wasn't the I-5. And Puppy had been driving a lot longer than Bron.

"Doesn't Kira's mom's place have a back gate?" Bron asked frantically.

"Yeah. I know where the latch is, too." Allen answered.

"Get us into the alley and I'll do the rest."

Bron dodged into a bank parking lot around a line of cars all backed up just to file their transactions through a plastic tube rather than having to walk inside and talk to a teller—a premonition of many things to come.

Ahead, Bron knew where there was a long street riddled with speed bumps. He led the chase in that direction then turned a second early between two houses. Bron slammed on the brakes and both boys hopped out to turn a dumpster sideways at the mouth of the alley. They saw Puppy blow past and head for the bumpy road they'd hoped he'd take.

Back in the Dart, Bron laid down black rubber stripes. With the time they'd lost and Puppy's truck jumping and clunking over concrete intervals, they were neck in neck at the first intersection. Allen stared out the passenger window and Puppy leered back in fury. Then both lost sight of each other as another block of houses blew by. That gave Bron just enough headway to reach the next intersection first. When he got there, he swerved hard right. Right toward the road that Puppy was on.

"What the fuck are you doing?" Allen asked in a panic.

"I don't know," Bron said. "Wish me luck!"

Puppy's truck came round the bend just then, arched hard left and headed straight for them. They were both picking up speed and the little paved lane was not a two way street. At the last possible second, Bron jerked the wheel. They ended up cutting two tracks through someone's freshly paved front lawn and popping an errant kiddie pool.

Puppy looked back over his shoulder then turned around to see that he was about to smash into a long row of metal garbage cans.

Bron jumped his car back onto the street and hooked around to the next smaller road that was out of sight. In another minute they were behind Kira's house and Allen was pulling the gate wide. Bron drove inside. The gate slammed shut and he killed the ignition.

Inside, Kira had a stack of her mother's books piled high in the dining room. She heard the rumble of engine in her back yard, jammed a bookmark in place and raced outside. She could see the fear in her friends and motioned them in quickly.

"Give you one guess," Allen said as they rushed through the screen and slammed it shut.

"Puppy?" she asked.

"And Bingo was his name-o," Bron mused.

The three stood with the back door cracked for a spell. After a minute, they heard the pickup rumble through the alley behind the fence. But it didn't stop. Its engine grew quiet as it drove into the distance, back toward the highway that headed south out of town.

"My mom's gonna be pissed about her yard," Kira said.

The back was a well-maintained garden with stacked stones, a Koi pond, and a year-round waterfall. Now a hulking steaming Dodge was parked in the middle of it all.

Bron apologized. "Yeah, sorry about that. I think she'd be more pissed if we got strung up and bled to death in the woods by Puppy though. Don't you think?"

"I wouldn't be too sure," she said. "Anyway, I'm glad you're here. We need to make a plan."

"A plan for what?" asked Allen. "For how to get this psychopath to forget he ever saw us?

"No," she said. "This is a lot bigger than Puppy. We have to help Rex."

"Who?" Bron asked, feigning ignorance. "Oh yeah, your boy…sorry. I meant to say, that commie dude who you spent the night with."

Kira just glared at him. Then, "He gave me the Resonator for a reason. Tomorrow we're going back out to Starr Creek to try it."

"Are you kidding me?" Bron was incredulous.

Kira looked over at Allen.

"Sounds like a terrible idea to me," he said. "Why on earth would we do this?"

"Because that…that Wendigo that we saw is real. And the Resonator will help us find it. And that's the key to all the weird shit going on in Starr Creek," she said.

"And why should I care about any of that?" Allen asked.

Bron crossed his arms and looked at her like she was nuts.

"Because," she said. "Puppy now knows your names, what kind of car you drive, Bron's license plate number, and most likely where you and your parents live. And if we don't do something quickly, we are all going to be in much deeper shit."

"Damn it," Bron said. "She's right. Why do you always have to be right?"

"Isn't that why you keep me around?" She smiled.

"So what do we do first?" Allen asked.

"We make a plan. We take inventory. We stockpile weapons. And we learn some spells." She waved her hand over the stacks of books on the table.

Allen nodded and took a seat at the head of the table. "All right. I know how this part goes. What level are we anyway?"

The clock on the wall chimed "one."

Kira frowned. Then told him the truth, "Zero."

22

Charles and Ethan suited back up into their Photon gear and remounted the trikes. Charles led the way again and they headed north up Bellfountain Road. After a mile-long straightaway the road split in two: pavement to the left, gravel to the right. Charles veered left and Ethan followed.

The grade of the road began to ascend toward the wooded hills beyond but Charles soon pulled off into a gated drive and parked. Past the gate was a wild wheat grass hillside. At its apex stood an oak tree with boughs that reached wider than those of any tree Ethan had ever seen outside of a storybook. He hopped over the fence in excitement then watched Charles casually unlatch the gate and swing it open. They were both still wearing their Photon get-ups but neither cared since this was a field, not a store.

At the foot of the great tree Ethan saw that wood beams had been nailed to the trunk to make a crude ladder.

"Up you go," said Charles.

"Why me?"

"Because I fall harder than you. And because you want those magazines, right?"

"Right."

Ethan found the rungs easy to cling to. He was up in the cradle of the oak in no time. Stowed in a hollow just out of sight was a package wrapped with twine.

Puppy sat watching from inside his truck across the gravel road on the other side of the fork. Once the scrawny kid made it up the ladder, Puppy got out of the truck and approached them.

"What do I do now?" Ethan asked.

"Toss them down here," Charles said.

Ethan dropped the package and scurried down the ladder.

"Great," Charles said. "Let's get out of here."

"Aren't we supposed to pay for them?" Ethan wondered aloud.

"Damn right," Puppy said, stepping out from behind the old oak's vast trunk.

Both boys jolted in surprise.

"What the fuck are you supposed to be, anyway?" Puppy asked.

"We're Photon," Ethan said with a shrug.

"Looks stupid," Puppy said.

"I've got your money, Puppy," Charles offered. "It's right here. Don't you worry." Charles pulled the crumpled ten out of his pocket and handed it to the man. "I also brought you some of these. As a bonus," he said, and pulled out a wad of tin foil.

"What you got in there, fatboy?" Puppy asked.

Charles unwrapped the foil, displaying a couple of white pills.

"My pa calls them oxies."

"Tell you what. I'll swap you," Puppy said with a smile.

He took two from Charles. Then he pulled a packet out of his pocket. He tore it open. Inside were two pills, small and round. Each had a cross grooved onto its face. He put one in each boy's mouth then pushed their jaws shut with a knuckle under each chin.

"You eat these and you ride on home. Real fast. Now get!"

Each boy swallowed the pill. They tasted disgusting, but far better than a beating from Puppy and they knew it. So Ethan jogged down the hill at the pace of Charles' run. By the time they got to the ATCs, Puppy was already peeling out on the gravel road.

"Are these like aspirin?" Ethan asked.

"I have no idea," Charles answered, short of breath from the run. "I hope so. Because I have one mother of a headache."

He set the magazines down on the seat of his bike and pulled the knot out of the twine. The brown paper wrapping fell away. Beneath was the shiny cover of the June issue of *Hustler*. It showed a woman standing in front of a grid of yellow ceramic tiles. She seemed to be taking a shower in milk. And she looked really happy about it.

Charles grinned in excitement at Ethan then flipped it open to see more. His smile faded when the cover slipped off, unstapled. The paper beneath was black and white. Yellowed pages crumbled with age at his touch. There were no photos of women or centerfolds. Just a bunch of dumb old stories about aliens and monsters and scholars going insane.

"That crook!" Charles shouted.

"I saw which road he took," Ethan said. He drew his Photon gun from its holster.

"Yeah. Me too. Let's play tag."

23

Charles and Ethan pushed their Hondas hard. They flew over grassy knolls and bounced around tufts of sedge that stood in triumph where winter sloughs had soaked the earth a few months prior. They rode through a lightning crackle of ravines that kept them off the road but just in sight of Puppy's truck. The pickup dozed its way up a stratum of gravel that kept a slacking pace oblivious to its place in the race.

Exhilaration broke the cross tops down in the boys' bloodstreams that much faster. They white-knuckled their rides and survived twists and turns that only the first generation of video gamers could muster without any actual training. They were *The Last Starfighters* of ATCs that afternoon. Their fear washed away in a fit of dynamism fueled by that first amphetamine rush.

Charles felt mad with power for the first time in his life.

NATHAN CARSON

His pupils were pinned and the trike handled his weight like a jet ski blazing waves in molten dirt. He looked ahead and saw the hairpin in the gravel road. This was his chance to cut off Puppy and serve justice just as his heroes did in comics and on film. Charles Leif bore the names of Kings and Vikings both. He was the son of the man called "Scary" by the mid-valley's most dangerous gang. His uncle Willie was in Angel's Harp too. Men quaked in fear when they heard that hoard of bikes growl into town.

Ethan saw it first. Charles was picking up speed in a sandy irrigation ditch that ran the length of the field. Between the trench and the county road Puppy unwittingly fled down, something low to the ground sprinted a beeline between them. It looked like a dust devil and parted everything in its path at a speed that seemed impossible for any critter Ethan had run across in his eleven years as a native Oregonian.

Charles saw the half-culvert ahead and knew that with a little luck he could use its steel curve to shoot into the road. In his mind he envisioned a landing either on the hood, windshield, or right into the bed of Puppy's pickup. That's what Face from the A-Team would do, he figured. He didn't have a plan from that point on but surprise was key.

Puppy's truck rambled down the road, swaying slightly from gravel path to dusty rut. He glanced onto the bench seat beside himself to snatch a glimpse at the open centerfold from the coverless magazine he'd kept. When he looked back up, a dust devil seemed to dance right over the hood of his truck followed by a 3-wheeler catching impossible air that arced overhead and out of sight. Puppy stomped on the gas and shot around a bend into the thick woods of Hell's Canyon, which were the rear entrance to his Starr Creek domain. Once he was out of sight, no one seemed to follow.

Charles cursed and flailed in mid-air. He'd misjudged the angle of the culvert and flew far higher than he'd hoped. In that dizzying moment he felt lighter than air. His stomach plunged down into his socks. The sun flashed in his eyes, blinding him. He heard Puppy's truck spinning its wheels on gravel and shooting forward. Then with a tremendous thump he landed on a bump and against all odds came sliding to a halt on the other side of the way.

There was a peal across the valley as loud as thunder but it resounded more like a howl of feral pain than any cloud collision.

Ethan buzzed across the road and skidded up to Charles to check on him. The pill was making him equally anxious. He leaped off the trike and shivered at the strange sound, the stress of the chase. Charles flung off his Photon helmet and let it drag behind him, still attached on a long cord by his holstered ray gun. His lip was bleeding badly from where he'd bit it, but he just wiped it away with the back of his hand and backtracked to his landing spot.

"Are you okay?" Ethan asked.

"What did I land on?" Charles asked without answering. "Did you hear that sound or was it in my head?"

"I heard it," Ethan said. "But I never heard anything like it."

They both frantically stumbled to the spot where Charles' trike had scored the dirt on impact. Dust still danced as if a bird was fluttering or an anthill had been angered. But there was nothing to see except for the disturbance itself. Then they heard it again, only softer. Pain. Animal agony.

It ripped through their guts in a primal way that made them recoil and peer closer as one.

"Do you see what I see?" Charles asked.

Ethan did. There was nothing on the ground. Except for a shadow of something neither boy could otherwise visibly detect, despite the broad and clear afternoon daylight. And there was no mistaking the grunts and gasps and skittering. It moved like an injured rattlesnake. But there was no snake. No rattle. Finally, Ethan picked up a cake of dirt, crumpled it toward the fineness of sand and flung it at the spot. Some bounced, some stuck, but there was certainly something there that was writhing and alive. It hissed when the dirt hit it but only fled in a broken circle, as if unable to escape.

"Hmm," Charles thought aloud.

His hands were shaking. The cross top helped him stay mad instead of fearful. He should have landed on Puppy, not on this, whatever it might be. He fought the urge to run up and kick it. But the phenomenon was too mysterious to attack without further study. Finally, he wandered back to his ATC and found his water bottle.

"Get yours too," he said to Ethan. It was an order.

Charles pulled in his helmet by the slack of its cable and reset it on his head. Then he got on hands and knees and started scraping the softest dirt into a pile. Ethan helped him and soon they had a small volcano of topsoil with a crater in the middle. Charles pulled the thermos open with his teeth and dumped the water onto the dirt. Ethan did the same.

Years of rock fights had made both boys a keen aim. With a dirt clod, a slingshot, or a pebble from the road, each could hit a stationary target this close with little trouble. They took handfuls of mud and slung it with unerring accuracy. Each time it hit, the creature staggered and sputtered, but never flew. And as patches of brown caked onto its outline, a form grew. Something the size of a small dog but shaped more like a bundle of mushrooms hunched on two stalks bent like chicken thighs. One leg was terribly broken from the impact of Charles' landing. Worst of all, it began to speak.

"Earth warriors. You are the first to tame us. We are humbled. Gah, the pain! Use your weapons. End us now."

Ethan and Charles looked at each other in puzzlement. Then Ethan drew his Photon gun and pointed it at the beast. It tried to scurry away but was too shattered to flee.

"What makes you think that we want you dead?" Charles asked it.

"Our watch was near complete. Our relief overdue. You have finished us. We can expect no help. Be done. Your cruelty prolongs our torment!"

"I'm sorry for running you over. It was an accident. Seriously. Listen, I have something good for pain."

Charles fished in his pocket, found and unfolded the foil. He drew a single Oxy out and inched toward the thing. It quivered but it did not lash out. Charles dropped the pill near it and sprang back.

"What is this thing? What has it gots in its pocketses? I have seen this on the screen with Squirrel. Is it a ring, precious?" The creature seemed to ape Gollum's animated television voice with precision.

"No dummy," said Charles. "It's a pill. You eat it, and it makes the pain go away."

The thing dragged itself within reach and clutched the Oxy in its blackened, mud-caked claw. It seemed to ponder its predicament for a moment. An invisible tongue licked at the pill. Licked again. Then the Oxy disappeared with a crunch.

Ethan and Charles stood there quivering with speed and watched the thing tremble in pain as the mud dried and flaked away. After a few minutes it started to settle and sighed with relief.

"Yes. It does work. Th. Th. Thank you," it said.

The boys got excited and smiled.

"I'm Ethan. And this is my friend Charles. We are really sorry that we hurt you."

"Your strike was...unintentional?" the thing asked.

"For sure!" Charles said. He could feel his heart beating in his wrists and his ankles. It reminded him of when he'd drunk a whole 32oz. Mountain Dew by himself and couldn't sleep all night. He could smell his unpleasant sweat.

"More," the thing said in its croaking inhuman voice.

So Charles ceded the last three pills. They disappeared in a flash. He wadded up the foil and dropped it where he stood.

Ethan's mind raced, tracing over the last hour. They had been chasing the scariest backwoods stranger he'd ever seen—a guy who called himself Puppy and sold porn to elementary school kids. His best friend ran over a creature that could talk but couldn't be seen. He'd been drugged with something he didn't know the name of that made him feel like the Flash from DC Comics. But there was really one thing at the top of his mind.

"Charles," he turned toward his friend. "I did what you

asked. I came with you. I made the trip to Bellfountain and I got up in the tree. Those magazines you promised are still mine, right? Even the one with Ozzy?"

Charles looked at his friend and shook his head. "That's what you're thinking about right now, you little perv?" He laughed out loud and then laughed some more and doubled over. He laughed until he coughed and spit and then he grew hoarse and teary-eyed. "Yes, Ethan. They're all yours."

"Good. A deal's a deal," Ethan said.

"Ahhh," the thing said, moaning with relief. "How long does it last?"

"I'm not sure," Charles said. "But some people take them every day. So I guess not more than 24 hours."

"Will you us bring more?" it asked.

Charles stood silent.

"It's only fair," Ethan said. "You ran him over. It's your responsibility."

"We can take turns," Charles said. "This was a group effort. You're just as wrong as me."

"Fine," Ethan said. "I'll come back. I'll never forget this spot." Addressing the thing, he asked, "You won't go anywhere, will you?"

"Cannot. We are broken. But the pain is gone. Do not let it return," it pleaded.

"We won't," Ethan promised.

Both boys started up their trikes again and pulled up alongside the creature, which was getting harder to see by the minute as the mud flecked off and the sun fled west.

"We'll be back tomorrow," Ethan said.

"Thank you," the creature said.

"What do we call you, anyway?" Charles asked before they sped off for home.

It paused in silent reflection. Then said, "We have no name as you would understand it. Though we have been called many things by those who feared us. But the one who cares for us most calls us...Babb-E."

February 29, 1960

Bonnie rode shotgun. Pregnant to burst, fluid ran down her legs on the passenger side of the truck's bench. She clutched her double barrel, balanced it on her throbbing belly. Between her teeth was a scrap of leather. She bit hard to contain her anger and fear. Anger at the thought of giving her babies life anywhere but the property. Fear of the doctors' sinful touch.

The neighbor man drove. He wouldn't hear of her dying in a childbirth gone wrong. Bonnie was blessed with twins and they were all twisted up and screaming inside her. He'd known her long enough to let her keep the gun.

Good Samaritan Hospital was still on Harrison Boulevard then. Bonnie was propped on a wheelchair and pushed through the doors with the shotgun still on her lap. A hush fell over the waiting room when they saw her. An orderly tried to calmly disarm her. He ended up planted on his ass, both barrels in his face. The stalemate might have gone on for hours but the pain caused her to seize. She dropped the gun, which fired as she hit the floor writhing. There was blood and broken glass and a ringing bell.

When she woke in the hospital bed a day had passed. Her first time in clean white sheets. She hated the smell of bleach. The stitches up her belly ached. The drugs tubing into her arm made her woozy. None of it mattered when they brought out her babes. A boy and a girl. To the nurses, they were a fright. To Bonnie, they were angelic.

She named them on the spot, made her mark on the certificates, and cradled them close. Her breasts were swollen with milk. She was happy that someone besides her grandfather was finally paying attention to them. Kitty suckled one and Puppy the other.

Bonnie was handed a bill for damages on her way out. After another kerfuffle, she was given back her gun, tagged and wrapped in plastic. She piled her newborns and her weapon into the cab of the truck. As the driver pulled out of the hospital lot, she took a good look at his smooth skin and widow's peak.

"You're a good man, Rex," she said.

November 1, 1975

The only other time Ma Tyler left her own property, she was behind the wheel. She had her own truck. Her shotgun hung proudly on its rack. And in the bed behind was the mountain lion she kept on a chain. She'd named it Goose.

Kitty had come home giggling drunk the night before, sobbing and laughing and making little sense. In the morning her head split, but she remembered. Puppy had got himself into a spot of trouble. She thought he'd find his own way home but he hadn't.

Ma screamed his name and fired in the air but he didn't come around.

Kitty gave directions from the passenger seat. She was reluctant but her Ma took no guff. They were on a rescue mission. For family.

When they rolled up on the fraternity house, a square-jawed young man in sweatpants sat on a couch on the front patio nursing a can of beer. His eyes opened wide when he saw the cougar in the back of the truck. They opened even wider when Ma Tyler blew a hole in the front door of the frat house with her double barrel.

In the dark and leaking basement, Puppy sobbed in a pool of blood. His transgression was never named. Ma and Kitty helped him up the stairs and into the truck. The frat boys' mouths were as bereft of words as their minds were of thought. They just stood there, finishing off last night's booze while they watched the Tylers cruise on south toward home.

Pedestrians gaped at the scene as the truck and the family and their big cat cruised down Third Street. A photo ran in the next morning's *Gazette Times*. But no charges were brought and no police visited Starr Creek Road that year.

24

Ethan felt his eyelids drooping on the ride home. He'd had so much energy all day. Now he felt drained as he could ever recall. The sun wasn't even quite set, yet he could have drifted off in his seat. But the ATC roared beneath him and they still had a few miles to go before they got back to the Leif's place.

Charles still led the way a few car lengths ahead. They had just hopped out of a western field and let their tires grip the pavement of the old Highway 99. Ethan saw Charles flag his arm to pull over so he followed his friend into the gravel of a driveway that bridged a steep ditch.

"What's up?" Ethan asked.

"Gotta piss," Charles responded.

Ethan kept his seat with the engine idling while Charles climbed down into the brush and trees below the road. A log truck grumbled past and the coiled cord of Ethan's

Photon rig danced on the breeze of night air in the truck's great wake.

"Hey!" Charles yelled. "You better climb down here and see this."

Ethan reluctantly killed the engine and took off his helmet. He yawned, rubbed the sleep from his eyes then dismounted. The hill was steep. The gravel made it treacherous. But Ethan had grown up in this terrain. He had footing sure as an eleven-year-old could command.

At the bottom of the hill was a deeper ravine that Charles was prodding with a stick. Ethan saw a silver and black blur of motion. When he got closer he could see the wheel of a motorcycle spinning freely.

"Wow," Ethan said.

"Yeah," said Charles. "Wow, alright. This is my uncle Willie's bike. I don't think he ran off."

"Is his body underneath it?" Ethan asked, hoping that whatever the answer, they'd be leaving soon.

"Not that I can see. And he's a big guy. Pretty hard to miss. Help me out here."

Ethan knew what was coming next and sighed. Being slim and fleet footed around Charles had somehow become the curse that volunteered him for every task Charles didn't want to commit to personally.

"Climb down there and grab the key, will you?"

The bike was upside down, propped between two jagged rocks. Getting beneath was little trouble. Ethan reached up and twisted the key in the ignition. The whole bike swung sickeningly toward him and fell, landing on another outcropping just inches over Ethan's head. He nearly wet himself. When he uncrossed his little twig arms from over his head, he wrested the key loose and scurried back up the bank. Charles reached his stick down to Ethan and pulled him up the final slope.

Ethan handed his friend the key. "Can we go now?"

The sun was sinking so they fired up the lights on the trikes. Dusk was not the safest time to be on the road; they kept one wheel on the gravel bank the whole ride back just to stay out of traffic's way.

Ethan felt elated as they rounded the corner by The Boog and raced up Church Street. He had spent the last three miles imagining the softness of his sleeping bag and the couch cushion pillow that he borrowed from the Leifs whenever he visited.

Charles got to the carport first and skidded to a halt. His dad's Harley was parked there. The second Charles turned off the engine on his ATC the front door to the house kicked open and out came Jerry Leif.

"What in the fuck do you think you're doing?" he screamed at his son.

Ethan rolled up just then and Jerry yanked him off the trike by his arm.

"And you, you little lying sack of shit. I've been on the horn with your parents. They are none too pleased."

Charles' face was the mask of a zombie. He'd already retreated deep within because he knew what was coming.

"I'm sorry, Dad. We went for a ride. I thought you were gone for the weekend. We were just having fun."

"You think it was fun for your mom and I to sit here for hours worrying about your sorry ass? You could have been anywhere, crushed to death. You think those toy helmets would do any good if you flipped? Guess again, buddy boy."

Ethan and Charles removed their Photon gear, embarrassed. They set it on a shelf under the carport and wheeled the ATCs to the back. In the shed, Charles made an effort to stash the bundle of magazines behind a cord of firewood that was stacked inside. When he turned to the door, Jerry was watching him and shaking his head. The elder Leif took three steps, reached behind the woodpile and produced the magazines. He held up the cover of the new *Hustler*.

"This is what you were up to, eh? Wait 'til your mother sees what a little miscreant she's raised. You make me sick."

"Dad, those aren't what you think. Look inside…"

He didn't get to finish because Jerry used the magazines to slap him across the face like he was swatting a fly.

"I don't want to hear it. What I do want to know is: who got them for you?"

Charles stood silent, tears leaking from his eyes and rolling over his rosy apple cheeks.

Jerry turned to Ethan. "You want to fess up here? I'll tell your folks it was a misunderstanding if you give me a name, boy."

That was the deal Ethan had been hoping for. "It was an Oakie named Puppy," he answered. "I think he lives up in Hell's Canyon."

Jerry Leif's mouth dropped open. "Holy sheep shit. You boys might have just bought your ticket out of hell. You think you can find Puppy? Everyone in Angel's Harp is itching to see him again." He turned to look down on his son. "Seems Puppy was the last one to see your uncle Willie."

That snapped Charles out of his mental retreat. "Dad,

we found Willie's bike." He fished the key out of his pocket and handed it over.

Ethan was slumping against the wall in exhaustion by now.

"Mr Leif, can I go home? Please?" He'd decided that whatever his parents did to punish him could not be worse than another night under the Leif's roof.

"Yesiree. I'm gonna make that call right now. And then a few more. Sorry, Jackie," he called into the house through its open door. "Looks like Country Fair's gonna have to wait 'til next year."

25

Saturday, June 21, 1986

Kira pulled the lemon yellow curtains open and Saturday morning sunshine poured in on Bron and Allen. They were sharing a blue futon that flattened into a bed in the guest room at Kira's mom's place. Allen sat up, squinting.

"Already?" he asked.

"It's almost eleven," Kira said. "And I think we are going to want as much daylight as possible out there."

She started fixing breakfast. Twenty minutes later Allen and Bron were seated at a clean wooden dining table as thick oat burger patties were set on little plates before them. Bron stuck his fork in one. It stood still as a flagpole in moon rock.

Allen took a bite. He might have been chewing unsweetened river rocks.

"Wow," he said. "This is what you eat?"

Kira shrugged. "They keep you regular. Want some honey? It's Fireweed."

"Yes please," both boys said at once.

After the dishes were cleared they started loading up Bron's car with supplies. He put his machete right on the dash in easy reach. Kira came out of the house with a leather and fleece kit slung over her shoulder. She set it in the trunk and then unfolded it for both boys to see.

"Whoa," Allen said. "Sweet crossbow."

"Thanks," she said. "I've had my eye on it for months. This morning I traded in some savings bonds and bought it."

"Do you know how to shoot one of these?" Bron asked. "It's not as easy as rolling a twenty-sided die."

Kira rolled her eyes.

"The guy at the shop gave me a lesson. I read the manual when I got home and practiced loading it while you were still asleep. I got an A in archery last semester. And my mom takes me to a shooting range. So, yeah. I think I'll be okay, Mr. Machete."

Bron held his hands up in defense and smiled. Then he opened the driver's side door, leaned the seat forward and waved her into the back. She climbed in while Allen unlatched the back gate. Bron did his best to baby the Demon's first gear to avoid peeling out on Kira's mom's victory garden. He was mostly successful.

*

On the drive south they schemed about the best ways to catch a Wendigo without being spotted by the Tylers.

"We know it runs the path near the Body Drop," Kira said.

"Yeah," said Allen, "And we also know that Puppy has a secret tunnel right next to that bottomless pit. I don't think that's a good place for us to hang around."

"Maybe the Wendigo uses those tunnels, too," Bron suggested.

All three of them shuddered at the thought.

*

By noon they were parked at the mouth of Starr Creek. Half a mile down on the right was a gaunt farmhouse, bleached white by the elements, paint peeling and shingles curling. Its tall black windows looked like the eyes of a dead man.

Bron pulled over into a tractor entrance by a stand of Christmas trees that were only a few months from harvest. They were just taller than the car.

Bron popped the trunk. Kira slung her crossbow over her shoulder. The weapon was small and sleek, black metal and wood grain. Bron threaded his belt through the sheath of the machete and wore it at his side like a sword. Allen stood in wait.

"Don't I get a weapon?" he asked.

"Did you bring one?" Kira asked.

"Hold on," Bron said.

He went back to the car and fished around in the glove box. A minute later he returned and put a Zippo lighter in one of Allen's outstretched hands and a little canister of breath spray in the other. Allen looked at his friend incredulously.

"You're joking, right?"

Bron said, "No way. Try it."

Allen flicked the lighter open and lit it. He shot a wintry blast of Binaca at the small flame and a plume of fire rocketed toward the nearest holiday tree. It caught immediately in the dry heat. All three of them raced to put it out and broke off the blackened limb before the rest of the tree could catch.

"Jesus. Okay, I'll hold onto these," Allen said, shaking his head.

"The last tunnel Puppy crawled out of was near here somewhere," Bron said. He was scanning the ground. After a few minutes he actually found the tracks from their skirmish. He traced them to the spot where he'd fallen. There was even a drop of blood to mark it. From there it only took the three of them a short while to find the canvas flap that obscured the entrance. Inside was impenetrably dark.

Kira motioned for them to sit. She drew out a number of small brass charms. She swung one like a pendulum in front of each of their faces. Another container was filled with a pink powder, which she spooned into her palm then blew into the tunnel entrance. It blew straight back out and into her mouth, causing her to cough.

The boys giggled at her.

"Well anyway, just trying to cover all our bases here," she said.

Then she withdrew a small vial that glowed even in the daylight.

Bron leaned in and stuck out his tongue. Kira shook her head.

"Not this stuff," she said. "This we are dropping directly onto our eyes."

Bron shrugged and lay down on his back because he was so tall. Allen watched as Kira squeezed two perfect drops onto his pupils. He blinked rapidly. When each eye opened, a pinpoint of white that looked like phosphorescent paint bloomed from the center until it took over the iris too.

"Cool," Bron said, looking around in amazement.

Ethan knelt in front of Kira and received his drops.

"Now you do me," she said to Allen. As a testament to their friendship he did not make a lewd joke in response.

He stood above her and squeezed out the remaining liquid into her eyes. Her pupils bloomed as well, but soon the glow bled beyond them and over the whole sclera. She blinked and her eyeballs emitted a light of their own. She took back the bottle and observed it.

"That was all of it!"

"Yes, I thought you wanted the rest," Allen said.

"That was enough for several trips," she said.

"Oh. Sorry."

They were silent for a moment as they adjusted to the vision. None of them felt the overwhelming mutation of reality that the ten hits had inspired. But their vision scanned the veins on nearby leaves like an x-ray. And they could see small animals foraging in the Christmas field many yards off, even though there were dozens of trees in the way.

Kira pulled open the flap and gazed into the tunnel. She drew a flashlight from her bag, clicked it on so that it shone down the tube. Then she clicked it off and said, "Follow me."

26

The night before, Squirrel had heard Puppy come racing back to camp in his truck. She wondered what kind of trouble he'd gotten into this time. What if the police did come? What if Puppy and Kitty were taken to jail? Where would she go? How would she eat?

She overheard Puppy telling Kitty his latest story. They both got a good laugh. He was trying to lose two boys on 3-wheelers that he'd ripped off for a couple of nudie magazines. He'd left the kids in the dust a few miles from Bellfountain. There was no way they could keep up with his truck and, so far as he knew, they hadn't even really tried.

The rest of the night was like every night at the camp. Satellite television, canned food, and drugged sleep to ward off the nervous energy of a gibbous waxing moon. The coyotes in the hills and woods around them were roving in anticipation. Even from the window, Squirrel could see fires on the hillsides of Starr Creek under midnight skies. Sometimes she wanted to run to them. But she knew better.

*

Everyone was in a strangely good mood the next morning. Over a breakfast of hash brown patties and Wonder toast, Puppy had broken out the pipe and foil. Squirrel got visibly animated. She slapped her hands on the table and gave a feral grin through clenched teeth.

Puppy pinched a little rock onto the foil and began to heat it from beneath over the butane flame. They took turns smoking and rushing. When each had their second round, Puppy dug through a drawer and produced a Bob Seger 8-track that only came out on special occasions. Kitty sat on a chair tapping her foot like a jackrabbit while Puppy and Squirrel danced around the kitchen knocking shit over.

Squirrel tidied up the house while the drugs passed through her system. She scurried from room to room grabbing things and putting them back where they belonged, constantly switching gears to focus on one project then another. She was making progress all over the place but nothing was really getting finished because she was too high to focus on any one thing.

*

By mid-day, she was dragging a bag of trash outside to the

burn heap when she heard a sonic boom split her world in half. She dropped the garbage where she stood. The bag split. Rotting food and all manner of grotesqueries spilled onto the ground. She fled back into the house, slammed the door, and hid in her room.

"I know it's to do with Babby," Kitty said. "Don't ask me how, but I just know it!"

She was hysterical. Puppy raised a hand to slap her face.

Her teary eyes just stared at him until he lowered his hand.

"Shut it about your damn Babby, sis. I'm going to check it out."

He reached toward the counter for the butterfly knife he'd taken from Bron and put it back in his pocket. Just as he was headed for the door he heard the alarm bell from the tunnel tripwire.

"On second thought," he said. "You look for Babby. I'm going under."

He was gone before she could protest.

"Squirrel!" Kitty cried. "Bring me my book."

Squirrel knew the one. There was only one, set in a room to itself where the tome was least likely to take damp. Its binding was black leather. The pages were thick and the writing made no good sense. She'd snuck in and tried to read it before but it was like trying to read the bible backwards while spinning on her pointy little head.

She gathered the book up in her arms like a child and brought it to the dining room where she laid it gently on the table. Kitty pinched her cheek then sent her away.

Kitty tried to remember everything her mother had taught her. She flipped through the pages of the book from front to back and scanned certain lines with her finger. Her lips moved as she read.

"I'm gonna need your help, Ma," she said aloud to herself.

"If I find you a virgin, will you bring me my Babby?"

27

Allen was having one of those special dreams. He felt a woman's hand cup his balls then stroke his shaft. He could even see the hand through his eyelids. That was how he knew he was asleep.

But then he remembered the Resonator making the tunnel walls crawl with fiery outlines. Kira had led them to a junction. She was peering down one path then the other. Allen took a step toward one and tripped on a tiny wire pulled taut across it.

"Why me?" he asked himself.

They all heard a bell ring somewhere far off, then silence.

Kira unslung her crossbow and carefully aimed into the distance. Soon they heard the measured boot falls of someone running. She stared with white glowing eyes into the darkness, let the runner get close and loud. When it seemed right on top of them she pulled the trigger. There was the twang of new string then the sound of a body falling to the ground hard. She and Allen and Bron fled down the opposite tunnel as fast as they could.

More junctions followed. And more strange sounds. The light and darkness started going crazy, making it difficult to tell which way was up or what tunnel branch they'd been down. More boots hurried in their direction. From afar, they heard the echoing bleat of what sounded like a goat. Then hooves on dirt grew louder and galloped closer than the boots. Allen's white eyes stared right into the red horizontal pupils of something inhuman; a blow to his forehead stole all light and reason.

*

Allen opened his eyelids and was unnerved to see the hand between his legs in full color. He was a sixteen-year-old virgin. A Doublemint gum commercial could make him rock hard. A gentle breeze on his neck. His Advanced Biology teacher. He let his gaze follow the hand to its bony wrist and scrawny forearm. Up the flabbiness that followed, past the neckless visage curled the grin of Kitty Tyler.

Allen started to scream. He'd been planning this moment for years. There were so many ways it could go wrong. Premature ejaculation. A girl with herpes. A guy with herpes. Sex was always going to be a risk for the greatest reward. But this…this was a fate he had not considered. Kitty stroked him all the faster. He was a helpless puppet in her nimble hand.

In an effort to blot out what was happening he took in the rest of the scene. He was tied to a post, nude from the waist down and standing. It seemed like a big room, somewhat how he imagined Hrothgar's mead hall in *Beowulf.* There were torches lit and a throng of beings he could not discern standing along either side.

He tried to let the embarrassment of the situation deflate him. But this was the first time he'd felt another human touch him in this way. Her hand was no dream. Concrete flesh stroked his desperate organ rapidly and with purpose. Awful. Inconceivable. Yet he felt the pressure mounting and the inevitability if Kitty kept on.

"Easy boy," she said. "Save it for the Black Goat."

She slowed her strokes a touch. The gates at the far end of the hall opened. Allen again heard the bleating that had resounded down the tunnel before he blacked out. This could not be happening. No amount of drugs or role-playing had earned him a bad trip of this magnitude.

The rows of figures parted, leaving a channel for the goat to approach. Allen had grown up with goats. He saw them as intelligent, gentle creatures. The one time he'd even let himself, for the sake of science, even consider one as a sexual object, it had expelled a few dozen raisin-sized pellets from its ass, which immediately cured him of further curiosity.

This thing was no earthly mammal, perhaps the size of a boar. Its horns curved like the head of a wicked Egyptian god. Its skin was blackened fur and wrinkles. The twisted knots of muscles buckled and rippled as it walked. Growths protruded everywhere. Wattles hung from its jowls and pink cysts sagged out from betwixt its dark, folded flesh. Everything about it reeked of age and decadence and evil.

At last, the Black Goat approached the dais on which Allen was being prepared. Once again he saw the cruelty in its pupils, each a tiny flame that danced in the center of its bulbous rheumy eyes. That misshapen head tilted slightly. Then the mouth broke into a smile that was all too human. And Allen knew then that whatever this was, it had not been born a goat.

The thing turned around and surveyed its flock. All heads were bowed. The torches flickered. Kitty resumed the speed of her strokes as the Black Goat backed up toward Allen, prepared to receive his virgin seed.

28

Ethan woke in his own bed on Saturday. Normally he set an alarm so that he didn't miss *Transformers*. This was one week that he'd have to borrow it on tape from a friend. It wouldn't likely be Charles.

He dressed and walked out to the living room. His parents were in the kitchen drinking coffee and reading the newspaper. Ethan had passed out on the car ride home the night before. So they hadn't really talked yet.

"Good morning," he said, sheepishly. "Am I grounded?"

His father looked at his mother as if to ask the same question.

"Yes," she said.

"Ok." Ethan sighed and let his shoulders droop.

"You're not to play with or speak to Charles for two weeks. He's a bad influence on you."

"Oh," he said. "So, I can still go outside and play?"

"Of course," she said. "Just not with Charles."

"Deal," he said. "Thanks, Mom." Then he opened the cupboard and poured a bowl of corn bran and tried not to smile.

After an hour of boring television, Ethan had a nagging feeling. He knew he was supposed to do something today. He walked back into his room and looked around. His backpack sat on a small wooden school desk. He unzipped the bag and found the magazines that he'd smuggled away from Charles. He quickly zipped the backpack and stashed it behind his winter clothes in the back of his closet.

The magazines made him think of Puppy. And then he remembered.

"I'm going for a bike ride," he said on his way out.

His parents nodded and told him to be careful and have fun, just like they always did.

Before he went outside, he stopped in the bathroom by the back door and checked every drawer and cabinet for anything that resembled the Oxies that Charles had. Nothing came close. There was cold medicine and there were vitamins. The only thing he could find for pain was Aspirin. So he folded a couple of those into a scrap of foil. Then, in case that wasn't enough, he jammed the whole bottle in his pocket and went outside.

His bike was spray-painted gold and had a black banana seat. It leaned against the side of the house. The seat and grips felt warm from baking in the sunlight. He mounted it and coasted down the gravel driveway toward the first big hill.

Many times he'd ridden down this decline and ended up curled in the blackberries at the bottom. It seemed that his bike's chain loved to come off its sprocket. He'd catch amazing speed and hit a bump in the road, which sprang him over the handlebars and into the bushes. Today he was on a mission. The bike rode smooth and shot him out onto the pavement of the main road like a golden bullet.

He knew the back road to Bellfountain. He'd ridden it before to check out library materials from the Bookmobile that parked by the old school every other week. The aging equipment in the schoolyard there was built at the turn of the century. It looked like a cross between a set from *Little House on the Prairie* and a bunch of medieval torture devices. Wood seats cracked into splinters. Rusting bolts jutted out in odd directions that seemed unsafe for children. Yet the utilitarian nature of those bolts held the damned things together long after other school districts had switched to plastic lumber and softer sawdust.

Ethan pedaled past the school up Bellfountain Road. An hour passed and his legs started burning. Normally he rode this far for leisurely fun. Or his dad would drive him to the top of a big hill and let him coast down. This was more like work and he wasn't built for it. He started missing the 3-wheeler pretty badly when he came into line of sight with the long hairpin curve.

From this distance he couldn't see many signs of life. A heron circled then landed on a stump by the road. A line of small beetles clacked across the blacktop's bright yellow centerline. Ethan took a drink from his water bottle, capped it. Then he got back on his bike and took the final stretch on pavement.

When he reached the culvert, he wondered if all of yesterday had been a dream. Or maybe a fever vision from the pill that Puppy had made him take. He also half-hoped that Babby might reveal great secrets to him. There was something about talking to a monster that made him feel very special.

He laid his bike by the side of the road and climbed down into the field. In another moment he'd found the cracked dirt where they'd left the creature. He couldn't see a damn thing so he called out for it in case it had crawled off somewhere nearby to die.

"Babby!" he called to the wind. "Babby, it's Ethan! I brought you something!"

At first it just sounded like a car in the distance. But soon the throat-rattle crescendoed into something awful. Ethan covered his ears to block it out. Then a few blades of grass rustled in the corner of his periphery. He hurried over to them and dropped to his knees. Most of the mud had fallen off and he could barely make out where the beast was huddled.

He reached a quivering hand out and set it on Babby's warm and glandular side. The moan it emitted ceased. Ethan could feel it inflating and deflating as it drew labored, painful breaths.

"Ethan?" it said. "Ouch."

"Don't worry," Ethan said. "I brought you more pills."

"Thank you, Ethan," it said.

He got excited now. He had just petted something inhuman that knew his name and calmed at his touch. This was so much cooler than the herd of guinea pigs he had raised that were later eaten by the neighbor's dog.

As he dug around his pockets feeling for the foil, his mind reeled at all the questions he would ask Babby today. It seemed to have lived a long time. It must know things other people didn't. Maybe Babby was like the Loch Ness Monster or Sasquatch. Or maybe from outer space. Had it once been human? He was going to find out all this and more.

Finally he produced the wad of foil from his pocket and uncurled it. Two white tablets dropped onto the ground. He pushed them with a fingertip right up to where he imagined Babby's mouth was. Even in broad daylight the thing was nearly impossible to see.

A few shards of dried mud revealed where its one usable appendage reached for the pills. It dragged them to itself and then they disappeared. The moment they were gone, Babby's whole body turned opaque grey as if it had frosted over in winter. Ethan caught a brief glimpse of the thing. Then it seized up and collapsed into a chalky dust that blew away in the wind.

29

Allen lost control the moment he entered the Black Goat. Kitty shoved him in with her palms on his bare ass. In one swift pump of relief and humiliation, he was done. Just then, the door at the far end of the hall opened, letting in the light of day.

Allen blinked. In that split second, the hall was cleared. No goat. No worshippers. No torches. Just a barn stacked with hay. He was standing atop a pile of alfalfa bales with his drawers dropped to his ankles and his pecker jutting out. Standing in shock just outside the barn door was Marnie.

Allen dropped to his knees, fell sideways, and did his best to get his pants up over his privates before she could cross the barn. By the time she reached him, he was shivering with fever and sweat. Marnie knelt down and put her hand on his forehead to feel his warmth.

"This…isn't what it looks like," Allen said. He couldn't

imagine a worse person to have walked in on him during a more confusing time.

"I don't know what you were doing," Marnie said, with kindness in her voice. "But I saw that terrible Tyler woman slip out the back as soon as I came in. Our family has had trouble with them since before I was born. You don't have to explain yourself to me. Come on. Can you walk if I help you?"

Inside Marnie's family farmhouse, Allen found himself tucked into her overstuffed bed. Her room was filled with elegant animal toys and inspirational posters trimmed with lace. She was a blossoming fourteen, but still surrounded by a childhood that was exotic to Allen who had no sisters. And what he knew of Kira's personal life was nothing like this.

Marnie brought in a white cozy soaked in cool water. She removed his glasses and set them on her nightstand by her white and gold telephone radio alarm clock, then laid the cloth across his forehead. He began to relax, but still felt utterly embarrassed and mystified over what had happened in Marnie's barn. As he gazed around the room he could only catch the slightest hints of afterglow from the Resonator.

"Marnie. Look into my eyes. Do they seem normal?"

She stared at him as if seeing him for the very first time.

"There's a tiny white spot in the middle. Do you always have that? I never noticed at school. But then, you always have your glasses on."

"No. Just today. And they'll probably be all the way gone soon.

"Listen," she said. "About the other night."

"Don't worry about it. I get it."

"No you don't," she said. "I really wanted to come meet you. But my sister ratted me out to my parents and they wouldn't allow it. Meeting an older boy in a graveyard at dusk is something they pretty seriously frown on. I should at least have called you, but the whole thing was very dramatic here. Anyway, I just want to say that I'm sorry."

Allen's mind was blown. This was almost weirder than the rest of his week. Almost. He took her hand in his and she let him.

"Maybe," he said, "I can take you to the mall next time? Or a movie?"

"I'd like that," she said.

She turned to browse through a white wicker chest full of cassette tapes. Allen took the opportunity to fish a few things out of his pants pockets. He took a quick hit off the Binaca Bron had given him to freshen his breath. And he used the Zippo to light a candle on Marnie's nightstand. The scent was snickerdoodle.

Marnie slid a tape into the deck. When the sounds of The Judds issued forth, she took a honkytonk dance step toward Allen and her bed. They both smiled for different reasons. Then a sonic boom cracked across the sky and her bedroom window shattered.

30

Ethan looked at the foil in his hand and dropped it in horror. Apparently Babby reacted badly to Aspirin. He dropped to hands and knees and tried to sift the powder that was left of Babby, but most of the creature had broken down and evaporated in a matter of seconds.

For a few minutes he just sat there wondering what the hell else to do. Clouds began drifting overhead, leaving him in shadow as the sun was veiled. Finally, he collected what little was left of the Babby powder, pinched it into his palm and snorted it.

Then the sky cracked in half and a gargantuan trapezoid of negative space burst through the clouds.

Ethan stared straight up. All he could see through that shape was blue sky. Then a beam of rose-colored light shot down to the area where he sat. It scanned his bicycle and the spot where Babby had died. When it enveloped his body, the beam dwelt over him for an extra moment. It blinked off and the sound of engines firing blasted the valley and roamed in the direction of Hell's Canyon. Soon the clouds began to resume their shape and cling together to patch the gaping wound punctured through them.

If the beam had burned him or even treated him as a threat, he'd have run straight for the culvert. But clearly he was insignificant, harmless in the eye of the invisible machine. With a mixture of courage and curiosity, he picked up his bike, ran alongside it to get up to speed and hopped aboard.

This was the road Puppy had taken the day before. The peaks of the tree line ahead bent down as the great nothing cruised overhead. When it passed, they sprang back into place, fir-green needles swirling down like confetti.

Ethan pedaled on. There was never traffic on Hell's Canyon Road. If he'd had a map he would have seen the great green expanse that blotted out the intersection where Starr Creek and Hell's Canyon legally connected. But he had no map. He just followed the dotted yellow line and the sound of mechanized thunder.

Eventually the sound drifted deeper over the woods and away from the road. Ethan turned off onto a rutted dirt track that was more suited for combines than street bikes. Soon the way was too rough. A hand-built wooden fence intervened. Ethan parked his bike against the fence behind a stand of coastal ferns that grew wild there. He climbed easily between two knotted beams. As he did, his shirt caught on a splinter and began to pull and tear. When he reached back to free himself, he saw right through his hand.

Ethan stood there, puzzled. He looked through his hand

at the trees, the ground, the sky. He seemed to continue fading the longer he looked. But he felt as solid as ever. So solid that the great body crashing into him felt like a sack of bricks.

"Ow," he cried. "Let me up!"

A tall boy of high school age rolled off of him. He had long black hair and a denim vest. His pupils glowed in the darkness. As Ethan lay in the dirt, the older boy drew a machete and pointed it at him.

"Are you the thing that ran by us the other day?" Bron asked.

"I'm not a thing," Ethan said. "I'm following a thing."

"Well, you're hard to see. Just like the Wendigo was."

"What's a Wendigo?" Ethan asked.

Bron tried to explain it but didn't really have the right words. He wished that he hadn't been separated from Allen and Kira in the chaos of the tunnel.

Ethan said, "I think you mean Babby. Yes, I've seen him. Sorry to disappoint you, but...he's dead. I don't really want to talk about it. We were friends."

"Well this is fucking weird," Bron said. "Anyway, I don't think it's safe for you to be wandering around in these woods. There are a lot of dangerous people here. They're flipping out and they are armed."

"Is one of them Puppy?" Ethan asked.

"Whoa? You know Puppy? Maybe you aren't such a liability. I'm looking for him too. I can see you, but I'm guessing he won't be able to. C'mon. Let's find a weapon for you and get my friends out danger."

The two boys edged further into the wood. In the distance they could hear scattered shouting and the odd cracking of gunshots. And always, there was the omnipresent hum of the machine.

"Shit," Bron said after a while. "I think my sight beyond sight is wearing off. Or else you're getting fainter."

"It's probably both," Ethan said. "Your eyes aren't glowing like they were when you tackled me. Jerk."

"Yeah. Sorry about that. Hate to break it to you kid, but I'm scared shitless."

"Good," Ethan said. "Because I didn't bring any toilet paper."

Bron just marveled at him, then laughed.

"How old are you, anyway?"

"I'm eleven. But before you judge me, you should know a few things. I'll be in sixth grade in September. I own a collection of *Hustlers*. Yesterday I ate cross tops for the first time. It was pretty cool. And I'm the one who killed Babby. But it was an accident."

Bron shook his head in amazement and pulled out his pipe.

"Then I guess you're old enough for a hit of this," he said. He lit it, scorched one corner of the green, then passed it to Ethan.

Ethan had seen his parents smoke pot. It seemed like something boring old hippies did. But Bron was none of those things. So Ethan gave it a shot.

"No," Bron said. "You're doing it wrong. Here, watch me. You have to pull it into your lungs. Now you try. There you go. That's right."

Ethan sputtered and coughed and handed the pipe and lighter back.

"Thanks," he said.

"You're welcome. I just think we could use a calming influence. Because this place is dark and scary."

"Can you stop reminding me?" Ethan asked.

They continued on and the volume of the hum grew, swelling into a feeling of pressure rather than sound. The air felt thick with the vibration. Branches on the trees shook overhead. Soon they could see a bright light, the same rose color emanating from a clearing ahead.

The two crouched low and stole up to the edge of the clearing to get a better view. Standing far to their right was a half dozen men from the Tyler camp all waving rifles at the empty space overhead. They seemed to be arguing about whether or not to open fire. Finally one shoved the other and took aim at the sky. When he shot, the hum stopped dead.

The shooter turned and smiled at his fellows. He was ready to receive his congratulations. But all the men behind him started to recoil and stagger away. He turned back to look up and saw a great trapezoid of rose light shimmer into the space above the clearing. A colossal silhouette shaped like nothing human blotted it out then sprang to the ground. One gigantic elephant foot crushed the shooter into the ground where he stood and sank six inches into the earth below him.

"I can't see it. What does it look like?" Ethan whispered.

"It's like, a fungus colony, with chicken thighs for legs," Bron said. "It must be thirty feet tall."

"I think," Ethan said, "it must be Babby's big brother."

31

Kira's glowing eyes could see around the corners of the tunnels. Nevertheless, she didn't detect the hand that grabbed her arm and yanked her aside until it already had her. She whirled in the darkness and planted her crossbow vertically beneath the chin of her assailant.

"Easy, Kira," Rex said in the darkness.

He released her and struck a match. Now she could see his face reflecting the glowing orange flame. The firelight temporarily killed her night vision and caused her white on whites to pulse and retract. Slowly, she lowered her weapon and let herself take a breath.

"Sorry," she said. "I got separated from my friends."

"This seems to be a habit of yours. Let's hope the best for them," he said. "But now, we have a greater purpose. My people are counting on me to lead them and you are my guide."

"What does that even mean?" she asked. "I've never been down here. You seem to know your way around. In the dark, no less. How can I guide you?"

"You have the vision, Kira. I see your eyes are activated. Now use them."

"What exactly am I looking for?"

"You will know. Look beyond. Do you feel it?"

The chaos in the tunnels was past. There were no more boots. No more hooves. No more screams. Bron and Allen had either escaped or been captured. So far as she could tell, only she and Rex remained below. As she scanned the periphery, she began to relax and stretch out. Solid rock walls had little to do with how the Resonator operated. And she had so much experience with hallucination and dreams that she was already quite comfortable with the idea of space-time as a highly subjective illusion.

"Go forwards," she said. "Always down and never left or right. I'm glad I brushed up on my Theseus last night."

"Lead the way, milady," Rex said. "I'll be your ball of yarn."

She marched down further into the burrows and wound and ducked under each raw overhang and clutching tree root. All seemed dug by human hands several decades prior. The path they took deeper had seen far less use than the one near the road where Kira had first entered with Allen and Bron.

Soon they reached another strata saturated with moisture. Drops of water clung and dripped from above; it ran in rivulets at their feet. They followed in the pitch and soon felt the teasing fingertips of a fresh breeze. Kira took heart at leaving the stale tunnel air behind. Still, she sensed that they were far below the surface and wondered just what might lie ahead. Something vast, her glowing eyes told her.

The glow was too overwhelming. Sensory crosstalk blurred into something too massive to discern. Then they rounded a corner and stepped forth into an enormous cavern.

"Well done, Kira," Rex said. "This is the place I have never been. Never found. And we have you to thank for all of it."

She still couldn't see him but she heard him remove a gun from the holster that hung from his belt. She gasped as she heard him pull the trigger. There was a sizzle of fire. A flare vaulted across the cavern and burst with fury into the air above.

Illuminated before them was a metallic clamshell the size of a fallen Ferris wheel. It hovered silently in space above the cavern floor beneath the stalactites that jutted from the ceiling. Rex and Kira took wordless steps toward it as the flare slowly decayed. When they grew closer, Kira could see that more than half a century of fungi was growing on the outer hull.

When they were just beneath it, Rex blasted another flare into the ground close by. Lichen sizzled and smoked.

"What is it?" Kira wondered out loud.

"It is our escape. And your glory. My people will make you a queen for this, dear Kira."

Rex raised one cupped hand and made a twisting motion. A thousand floodlights on the object burst into life. The clamshell's top and bottom seemed to pass directly through each other then stopped once the center ring was extended into position. The top and bottom shells began slow opposing rotations above and below. A drawbridge extended down to the cavern floor in invitation.

Kira aimed her crossbow at whatever might venture

down that plank. Rex laughed aloud.

"There's been no one aboard this craft in seventy-six years, Kira. We will be the first."

She lowered her weapon. He led her up the gangway into the ship. The interior was a writhing hive of lights and tubes so bright that, coupled with the Resonator, Kira was nearly blind. She let Rex pull her through the low and narrow passages. Her only other choices were to flee back to the tunnels or sit on the ground and abandon sanity.

Rex was not searching nor was he lost. He escorted her straight to a control room. Once there, he dropped to his hands and knees. All the instruments were designed for something barely a foot off the ground. In seconds, Kira felt gravity shift as the vessel prepared to move.

"You know how to fly this thing?" she asked.

He did not answer right away.

After a ponderous moment, he said, "The greater question is: how did it get underground and can we blast our way out?"

Kira looked up through the hull of the ship, through the stone and earth above. What she saw was a vast reflection of her own face smiling down at her. And then she knew.

"Rex. We're right below the lake."

"Are you certain?"

"As sure as I have been about anything that's happened today."

"Marvelous," he said. "And maddening. To think that we've been living atop it for all these years. Time to restore faith and rescue my dear people of Nemi."

Rex traced two fingers across some sort of magnetic strip. The ship lifted off. When it struck the ceiling of the cavern, alarms began to sound and screens burst to life. In the curved monitors that wrapped around the lower edges of the control room, Kira could see that stones were falling and waterfalls were gushing lake water onto the cavern floor below.

As the structure weakened, more and more stone gave way and crumbled. One puncture was so large that the water spilling into the saucer at the top of the ship caused their craft to lurch unsteadily to one side. Kira skidded across the room and fell into a bank of inexplicable machines. Rex kept focused on flying and soon righted them. Before long, they were rising again. There were a few moments of silence as they drifted through the languorous draining lake water. Then they burst into the sky above in whirling glory.

"Nice flying," Kira said.

She was unnerved that Rex knew how to operate something that shouldn't even exist. She was just as thankful that he could.

"Now how about some answers? Where are we going and what is the plan? I thought you wanted me to find the Wendigo?"

"That is no longer necessary. Seeking that creature was only a means to an end. You circumvented that nicely by leading me straight to the ship. There will be many chances to thank you properly. But for now we must load my people on board with haste. I've waited so long for this moment and feared it had already passed."

The screens were bright as windows, revealing a gentle June afternoon above the Nemi Commune. Kira was dazzled by the beauty and serenity of the grounds. But she was also nagged by concern for her friends and the fact that Rex was revealing so little.

She turned to question him further, but he was already at her side. He reached to embrace her when she noticed the crossbow bolt embedded in his side.

32

"You sure he took Hell's Canyon?" Jerry Leif asked his son.

Charles nodded. "At least, that's where we saw him last. After he headed into the woods we gave up chasing him. I didn't feel safe following him home."

"Smart man," Jerry said: a rare compliment.

"Thanks, Dad. So will I ride with you or follow on the ATC?"

"You're not going anywhere, buddy boy. You're still grounded."

"But Dad! I found Willie's bike. I told you where Puppy lives. I should be there to see this go down."

"Son, this is a matter for grown men. Angel's Harp business ain't got shit to do with you. I'm sending your mom back down to Minnie's. You can go with her or you can stay put until I get back. I don't expect it will take too long for the whole gang to sort this out. Puppy may be a slippery flea bag but he's a coward too."

"Aunt Minnie's place has that weird patchouli smell," Charles said. "If I stay here can I at least have a weapon? In case he comes back here to look for me?"

Jerry furrowed his brow. His pointed nose peeked through his bushy beard and mustache. His beady eyes unfocused then locked on his son.

"All right. Hold on."

When Jerry returned to the room he set a black gun on the dining room table. It looked like something military or a GI Joe action figure weapon grown to life size.

"Thanks, Dad."

The elder Leif suited up in his leather vest and went outside. After a hug and a squeeze he sent his waving wife south in her old Volkswagen Beetle. Then he climbed back on his bike to rendezvous with the rest of his gang.

As soon as Charles heard the bike round the block he immediately lifted the gun from the table. Sporting a huge grin, he opened the chamber. The smile left his face as he counted the cherry-red paintballs inside.

"Fucking double crosser," Charles grumbled to himself.

Leif may have been a Viking name, but days like today made him wish he'd been born to the Cooks or the Bakers. Or better yet, the Smith-Wessons.

He looked over at the TV. It sat cold and silent. He and Ethan had survived Puppy. They had wounded an alien. And they had both sold and eaten pills for adults. The only trouble they'd gotten in was from their parents. That clinched it. Eleven was grown up as far as Charles was concerned. He gathered supplies, locked up the house, and topped off the gas in the 3-wheeler. No one was going to make him miss out on the fireworks.

It took him about half an hour to get back to the spot where they'd left Babby. The grass fields were strangely silent. He spotted the clearing, but try as he might he could not locate Babby. The only things marking the spot were two crumpled up balls of tin foil. Ethan had obviously made it out here. Maybe he had taken Babby away.

Charles was considering riding straight to Ethan's from there when he heard the rumble of Harleys. He pushed his ATC behind a stand of nettles and dove down into the culvert.

Two-dozen choppers cruised overhead into the woods of Hell's Canyon beyond. As soon as they'd passed, Charles wheeled his bike out of the brush and aimed it at the road. He cranked it back on and followed his father where he'd failed to follow Puppy.

About half a mile into the woodlands Charles caught a gleam of gold on the side of the road. He pulled over and rolled up toward it. When he was a stone's throw away, he knew he'd been right. Ethan's bicycle leaned against a greying wooden fence. Charles rode the perimeter of the railing. He found a stretch that had been caved in by a fallen tree sawed into pieces but never hauled away. He slowly drove over the rotting barrier and retraced the way to where Ethan had hopped over. From there he followed a path deep into the trees.

For a while he feared getting lost in the great forest. The firs were mostly bare near the ground but their limbs stretched out and gripped one another near the top. The crisscross patterns of brown branch and green fir blotted out the sun. It could almost have been night.

Charles stopped his engine. The sound of the forest crackled. He hearkened and heard two things. Dead ahead was an ambient groaning in the sky like a factory had lifted off to float above the forest. To the northwest, on his left, he heard the sputtering and spinning wheels of Angel's Harp.

He wove through the trees until he caught sight of their headlights. They were angled in all directions. Some men were off their bikes, pushing. Jerry was at the head, trying to drive straight over a large tree that had been felled across the road. The trunk was too thick though. He ended up dropping his bike and hopping off in a fit.

Jerry stood on the fallen log and addressed the gang.

"This is fucking bullshit. These inbred fucksticks didn't just put up No Trespassing signs on public land. They booby-trapped it so no one could come out to spank them."

Another rider named Dudley said, "How about we take the long way around?"

"How do you figure?" Jerry asked.

"Well," Dudley said, "if we ride back out to Bellfountain, we can circle back in on Starr Creek road. It's supposed to connect to Hell's Canyon, except these freaks think they own the whole place. I can see how they gummed up the works on a back road like this. But Starr Creek's paved from what I remember."

Jerry stared at Dudley then donned his helmet again.

"All right, all right. Let's do this."

Then, as a pack, Angel's Harp retraced its path and headed back to Hell's Canyon Road to make the long loop around.

Charles chuckled to himself. There were many places an ATC could go that a dual barreled street bike could not. He climbed back on and cruised deeper into the woods toward the low, throbbing hum.

The going was not easy, even on three wheels. There was so much vegetation, fallen limbs, and jutting mossy rocks. In places, whole rusted cars slumped down hillsides like broken skeletons, overgrown with moss and fern. Charles was careful not to take any major risks. He needed to be able to ride home before his dad noticed he was gone. There was no way he could sprint nine miles without risking a heart attack.

Around another ravine and its border of trees, he heard gunshots. Flashes of light followed. Charles hopped off the bike again and ran toward the action. As he neared the edge of the clearing, he saw a figure fusing with the shadows. Beside it lurked another form. Though nearly impossible to see, Charles recognized some of Ethan's clothes clinging to its all but invisible frame.

Charles didn't want to imagine that Babby had eaten Ethan. But the only things he'd ever seen that looked like that were a mirage on the road, and Babby. He couldn't tell if the guy in the shadows knew that this thing was almost on top of him. Charles had never had a chance to be a hero before. He unslung the paintball gun, which was longer than a pistol, fully automatic, and held an extra clip that hung down like the beard of a pharaoh.

Charles took careful aim. Beyond his target, more shots were fired. There was a scream and the crunching of bone. A tremendous weight crashed into the earth and nearly knocked him off balance. He squinted at the sight, took careful aim just above the neckline of Ethan's shirt, and pulled the trigger.

A split second later, Ethan cried out. The back of his head burst into red as he dropped to the ground. Bron looked down and gasped. Then he scanned the periphery behind him to see who had felled the boy. A rotund kid with some sort of assault weapon was running toward him.

"I got him!" Charles yelled.

Ethan sat up and rubbed the back of his head.

"Ouch. Jesus. Why did you shoot me?" he asked.

Charles stopped a few feet away. "Ethan?"

"Yes, Ethan, you dumbass."

Bron wondered if the weed he'd just smoked was laced with something.

"How are you even alive?" he asked Ethan.

Ethan touched the back of his head and pulled a great glob of red paint out of his hair.

"It's not blood," he said. "It's paint."

The weirdest part was that Bron could barely see his face. But he could see the interior of the red concavity facing him.

Charles apologized again. "I thought Babby ate you and stole your clothes."

"Babby's dead," Ethan replied. "We have much bigger problems now."

Only the screams and commotion and beams of rosy light kept the three of them from being spotted.

"So, you two know each other?" Bron asked.

"Yeah," Ethan said. "Best friends."

"Okay, good." Bron nodded in approval. "Then I trust you two can work this out and stay out of trouble. I need to get to my car. I think if I can find my way into the tunnel system here, I can take a shortcut."

Ethan saw like Babby now. He scanned the ground.

"There's a hole right over there. In the bottom of that tree."

Bron checked it out and found that Ethan was right. He drew his machete then dove into the hole to sprint for his Demon.

33

Deep in the network of catacombs, Puppy was snuffling along another trail. He could hear Rex and the little spy-girl plunging deep into the earth beneath the commune. Puppy never came this way. For these were the first tunnels and led nowhere he wanted to go. The darkness was somehow thicker here. He pulled at his shirt collar as the old air choked him.

When he finally caught up with them, the open cavern was crumbling. Torrents of water flooded in. But so did daylight. Puppy could see the sky. He scrambled up the sides until the water filled in the cave and he was able to dogpaddle to the surface. When the broad daylight stung his eyes, he was treading water near the edge of the lake on the commune property.

Puppy could see all kinds of hubbub on shore. Masked hippies were stacking supplies and lining up near the walkway that led to something Puppy couldn't quite put words to. He'd seen flying saucers in the movies, but this one looked like it had turned itself inside out with salmonella. It seemed pretty obvious that he'd find Rex and the girl on board, though.

Puppy dove down and swam to the far side of the lake. The tide was very low because so much water had settled into the cavern below. It drained even further as he swam. Once he reached the edge, he pulled himself up the muck of the side by clinging to roots and slime-coated rock. On shore, he ran hunched to keep out of sight. There was a grove of trees between him and most of the activity. So he headed for it. Once inside, he pressed his back to the tallest tree in its center.

He could see that two figures stood guard at the grove's entrance on the other side. But their backs were to him. One was called away to some other duty. Puppy saw his chance. He looked up the tree and saw a dying limb jutting out just beyond reach. He leaped into the air and caught it. With his body weight he was able to break it off. In his hand it felt solid enough. He padded up to the lone guard and bashed her across the back of the head. As she crumpled, he pulled her into the grove and took her uniform and weapon.

Luckily, she had not bled much. Puppy donned the cowl and marched toward the plank to the ship. When he reached the base, a commune-dweller motioned for him to place his rifle in an ever-growing pile. He did, but no one asked him to drop the bough. He awkwardly pretended to use it as a walking stick and ascended into the floating craft.

*

Kitty scurried away from the backside of Marnie's barn. Venturing so far to hold a ritual of such importance had been a risk, but there was simply no structure on the property around the camp that could host all the believers who had camped nearby and prayed around their fires overnight.

The Black Goat should be very pleased with her, she thought. She had delivered. Virgin seed was spilled; only a matter of time now until their numbers swelled. But what about her Babby? The old one owed her a bent ear about their bargain. And she knew just where to find the beast.

The spot was marked nearby. Once Kitty found the entrance, she placed one foot on the cart and pushed it along the rails with her other. She rushed along the track, kicking and heaving to keep in motion. Even the crow couldn't fly so unobstructed in the forests above.

To pass her time in the darkness, she mused. Frets about Babby twisted into memories of the many fantasies that had been whispered into her ear from her Ma, the Book, the Goat. What a strange world. Kitty figured that few living knew more about True Nature than her. The elements were so powerful when ushered in the right direction. And her Babby had been a tiny lost stranger in the midst of it. The only one who could not be harmed by Earth's myriad natural defenses.

The cart passed a side tunnel that blasted like a speaker. Kitty kicked at the floor to gain speed as water rocketed into the tunnel behind her and split like a two-headed snake to search out whichever path was more beguiled by gravity.

Kitty felt her will slip. Doubt spilled in again. She knew that she was a novice and fool. The elements were not remotely under her command. At most, she hosted a pantomime of a ceremony she could never understand. She could have done without jerking off the boy. But those pats on the head from a dark goddess sure did make her smile.

A wall of water caught her from behind and pushed the cart ever faster. Kitty took a deep breath at the last second then the wave plunged her under. She held onto the cart as long as she could but eventually spun head over heels into the swell. Just as she was ready to succumb, the aqueous tendril spat her sprawling out of the tunnel by the house.

She skinned her knees as she skidded. But that was the worst of it. Kitty was glad to be alive, not least of all because her services were still needed. She huffed to her feet and staggered to the back door of the home where she'd spent her whole life. No wonder the woods beckoned.

At the threshold, she heard gunshots and men yelling in the woods behind the house. Kitty keened to discern what was happening. A coarse bellowing echoed from inside the house and eclipsed whatever had the men in frenzy. Kitty rushed to her room and threw open the thin wooden door on its one remaining hinge.

Inside there were robed supplicants kneeling around her bed. Draped atop the covers was the Goat. Its hooved legs straddled the width of the bed, leaving room for its swelling belly. A drove of smaller creatures crawled inside it, seeking a way out. Kitty could see them writhing and prodding at the stretching flesh.

Out the bedroom window, Kitty saw trees shaking and

Ethan lifted his head from Charles' lap and watched The Young feed on The Foot. He'd hoped the aspirin would do the job, but he knew better. It would have taken a truckload to put a dent in a creature this size. Now that he had some of Babby inside him, he could see that the great trapezoid in the sky was not a natural phenomenon. As The Foot struggled, its ship moved in closer.

Jerry was trying to rally his men when a bullet glanced his forehead. He dropped to one knee then swiftly rose again. A stream of blood ran down his cheek. He eyed the man named Turk and raised his weapon to fire in kind.

People who had lived on the property for years sought to protect it from an invasion of heavily armed bikers. Robed magicians were caught in the crossfire. Magic battled religion in the midst of a power far beyond either.

The Foot uttered a cry and buckled under the feeding horde. A green beam issued from the ship above. The Young squealed in their death throes. As the beam enveloped The Foot, Young shed off by the hundreds, dropping to the ground cold and still. In seconds none remained alive.

There were bullets flying everywhere. In the midst of it all, the Elephant's Foot still advanced on whoever came close. The body count was rising. Blood turned the dirt to mud. As the ground softened, a circulatory system of tunnels caved in at once. They were full of lake water and soon choked on the bodies of men who lost their footing too close to the edge. Behind the Elephant's Foot a vast chasm yawned open. All water that reached it poured into that gulf. As it drained away, camp men and bikers continued to take shots at each other from behind barricades and fallen bikes.

Charles had his eye on The Foot. He left Ethan in the bole of a tree and leveled the paintball gun at the focal point of the green beam. He screamed as he emptied the clip. By the time he was done, the gun clicked impotently. The Foot's barn-sized mushroom form dripped with red war paint. Otherwise, it stood tall, indestructible, seething with displeasure at all it had discovered of humanity. The Ukrainian radioactive wastes where it had earned its name were more civilized than these American backwoods.

Every man remaining fled. Their bullets were but an annoyance. The ceremony of the Black Goat had failed them all. A few wondered if there were words worth speaking. Many Angel's Harpers prayed—but what god could hear them over such a din? Then an engine roared up the gravel toward the property.

Bron pushed his Dart harder than ever. It had taken some time to reach the far end of Starr Creek but he was proud of his instincts. Even underground he had retraced his path with prowess.

Bron swerved around fallen Harleys and errant bodies. He aimed straight for the great beast. The Resonator was long burnt from his system. He could no longer see the thing; only the red bullseye that Charles had painted on it. Bron's black eyes scanned the ground. He spotted the arched hunk of roof from the house. Its shingled frame was shaped like a ramp.

There was no time to reconsider. Bron pushed the tape into his cassette deck and cranked "Disposable Heroes" at top volume. A little hearing damage was the least of his worries. His pentagram necklace hung on the rear view mirror for luck. He gunned the engine again. The Dart raced up the eaves of the grounded house and launched skyward.

The Foot saw a metal object hurtling toward it and prepared to repel the nuisance like it did all of mankind's toys.

At the same moment, Bron saw the fat kid on a 3-wheeler flying across his path from the opposite side. Charles had strung all his Red Rats together. They were already lit. He lobbed them at The Foot. Tiny firework explosions cracked like a spine, distracted the beast. It lost its balance. Charles crashed back to earth and rolled off the trike.

The Demon soared through the air. The second before it connected seemed to last forever. Then the rubber band of time snapped and the car collided with The Foot. With the weight of American steel at top speed crashing into its body, The Foot was bowled over backward into the chasm. Bron and the Dart disappeared over the side with it.

35

Kira reached out to touch the crossbow bolt that protruded from Rex's abdomen.

"That was you I shot?" she asked.

"Yes," he said. "I had meant to scold you for that."

"I'm sorry, Rex. It was so dark. I couldn't see you."

"Not to worry, Kira. I'm very hard to kill." He snapped the shaft off where it entered his shirt and dropped it to the floor. Then he swiped another control strip and spoke into a floating sphere that seemed to operate as a microphone.

"Attention, my people of Nemi. Once again, I thank you for your faith. When the comet passed us, it seemed that we would be shackled to the Earth for another seventy-six years. But the courage and vision of our new friend Kira has been our liberation. There is little time to waste. All of you, please prepare for the journey. Find a room and stow yourselves safely. We rendezvous with the comet and gather new coordinates soon. Let all our love be never ending."

"We're leaving...Earth?" Kira asked.

"Of course. You must read the news, Kira. Nuclear annihilation is imminent. The Star Wars Defense Initiative your President promised will never occur. The only haven is far from here. I'm so glad you can join us. Now please, go find a safe place to sit or lie. I can't be distracted."

The ship was already in motion. On screen she could see the grove by the now-dry lakebed shrinking below.

"But I don't want to leave. My friends are down there."

"Your friends who I never seem to meet and who you've always just abandoned. Why is that, Kira? I can tell you. You have a greater purpose than wandering in the woods with drug-addled teenagers."

"Hey, they're good guys. They're a lot smarter than you're giving them credit for. Anyway I'd love to know if they're still alive."

Rex zoomed one of the screens back toward Starr Creek. He and Kira gasped as they watched the Elephant's Foot swarmed over by the Young of the Black Goat. Above the fray was a great ship, trapezoidal and menacing.

"I've got to get back down there!" Kira cried.

"That's not going to happen. Go find somewhere to be. We leave the atmosphere in a matter of minutes."

Kira staggered into the hallway in shock. None of the Nemi people were to be seen. They had all secured rooms with something to hold onto. The ship was rising at an angle. Crossing the hall meant hiking a steep path. Just as she neared the top, a door opened beside her. A hairy hand covered her mouth and pulled her inside.

Kira fought and twisted but Puppy had more strength

and wiles by far, at least when it came to fighting. Finally she relented. That's when he let her go and pushed her across the room into the wall.

"Rex's taking us into outer space," he said. "That where you want to go?"

"No," she said.

She saw that he was disguised as a Nemi and brandished a large wooden bough stained with blood.

Puppy said, "Go back down there. Get him talking. I'll take care of the rest. My family needs me. And your little friends are probably missing you by now. Am I right, girl?"

"Okay. Just don't kill him. He thinks he's doing the right thing for his people. But kidnapping me was never the deal."

Puppy gave her a nod that meant they had an understanding and opened the door. Sliding back down to the control room was easier. Before she entered, Puppy handed her the butterfly knife. She recognized Bron's blade but didn't say so. She just gripped it and went in.

For a moment, she stood over Rex's shoulder, wondering what to say.

"Back already?" Rex said without turning.

"Yes."

"What can I do for you?"

"Well, for one, you could explain to me why I couldn't see you with the Resonator. Everything was so vivid and you were like, just a hole. A negative space. What's your secret, Rex? Why do they call you never ending?"

Rex chuckled to himself.

"Those are not the right questions."

"I shot you. Why aren't you hurt?"

"You're getting warmer."

"Are you going to sacrifice all your followers when we get to wherever we're going?"

Rex whirled around and stood tall.

"My people are my life. I would never do a thing to harm them."

"I don't believe you," Kira said. "I don't think you have a heart."

"You want to know that I'm human? I have lived a long time but I am a man. Is it blood that you want, Kira? If this will set you to rest, I'll gladly shed more today."

He offered his wrist to her. She stared.

"Go ahead. Satisfy yourself. We have no time to waste."

Kira sliced across Rex's wrist. The blade was sharp. Beneath the skin where veins should have been were wires and circuits. Kira dropped the blade in shock. Rex looked from his wrist to Kira and opened his mouth to speak. Before he could, Puppy raced into the compartment. With a brutal swing of the bough, he bashed Rex's head into a cluster of instruments. The ship tilted drastically and began to descend.

"Can you land this thing?" he asked Kira.

"Hell no!" she said. "Only Rex knew how."

They both looked down at the floor where Rex was sprawled. A lubricant fluid that was not blood leaked out of one ear and trickled into a small pool.

Kira got down on her knees and started touching buttons and throwing switches. The ship did a sickening flip then righted itself. Daylight was fading. She could see the rising full moon on screen, the black metal trapezoid of the other ship below. Finally she found a control that locked their course toward that other, larger craft. So far as she could operate the alien instruments, her choices were either that or the path to the comet.

"Hold on!" she yelled to Puppy. He gripped the wall and braced himself.

The screen showed an icon of the Foot's ship. There was a map that showed its trajectory from the Ukraine to Oregon. The icon started blinking. Kira could see beams of energy racing toward the ship she was trying to pilot. Automatic defense systems aimed to blast Babby's craft off its collision course. The rays struck. Explosions rocked from deeper within. Nemi communists screamed in terror.

Emergency systems snuffed the worst fires. Steam filled the compartments. Puppy stood over Rex's body. A group of Nemi people burst into the control room. When they saw Puppy, they dragged him away kicking and screaming and howling.

*

On the ground, Charles and Ethan stared into the sky as the closest ship took aim at the other hurtling toward it. When they saw the beams ignite, they started to run.

With a bellow of anger, the Elephant's Foot began to clamber out of the chasm. It flung the Dart into a nearby tree and swung its bulk back onto land. Backlit by sunset, the beast's silhouette was a barbaric scar, an unreal vision.

Kira guided her plummeting craft toward the ship that was firing on her own. She recited another Wiccan prayer then stopped short. Wherever Babby had come from was a power that shrugged off Black Goats and Diana's Mirrors like scarecrows in the midst of a field burn. Instead, she closed her glowing eyes. Beyond her eyelids, beyond the ship's hull and the planet's crust, she resonated with a billion billion stars twinkling in the infinity of space.

As the full moon rose on the horizon and the sun dipped away, Babby's craft slammed into the warship, its supposed relief. The two spiraled to the earth like a fireball into the Elephant's Foot and lodged in the mouth of the chasm. The resulting explosion leveled the whole camp. When the smoke cleared, nothing crawled from the wreckage.

ABOUT THE AUTHOR

Nathan Carson is a musician, writer, and Moth StorySlam Champion from Portland, OR. He is widely known as co-founder and drummer of the internationally touring doom metal band Witch Mountain, host of the FM radio show The Heavy Metal Sewing Circle, and the owner of the boutique music booking agency, Nanotear.

Carson's byline can be found on hundreds of music and film-related articles in outlets such as the *Willamette Week*, *SF Weekly*, Orbitz, *Noisey*, *Rue Morgue*, *Terrorizer*, *Metal Edge*, etc.

In recent years, Carson has turned his sights toward weird fiction, with stories published in acclaimed magazines and anthologies such as *Cthulhu Fhtagn!*, *Strange Aeons*, *Swords v. Cthulhu*, *Eternal Frankenstein*, and *The Madness of Dr. Caligari*. *Starr Creek* is his first book.

LAZY FASCIST 2016

Witch Hunt by Juliet Escoria

Rumbullion by Molly Tanzer

The Birds & The Beasts by Andrea Kneeland

Glue by Constance Ann Fitzgerald

Starr Creek by Nathan Carson